ECHOES

FROM

SADDAM HUSSEIN

George Thomas Clark

ISBN: 978-1-7332981-3-1 – Trade Paperback
Copyright 2017 by George Thomas Clark

GeorgeThomasClark.com
Bakersfield, California
webmaster@GeorgeThomasClark.com

Books by George Thomas Clark

Hitler Here
The Bold Investor
Paint it Blue
Death in the Ring
Tales of Romance
In Other Hands
King Donald
Obama on Edge
Echoes from Saddam Hussein

Introduction

With sharp satire and precise writing George Thomas Clark takes readers into the halls of power, and indeed into the minds of the powerful after the American attack on Iraq. Saddam Hussein and George W. Bush are at their deceptive best, and often unintentionally humorous as they attempt to justify their actions. Dick Cheney, Condoleezza Rice, Karl Rove, Mahmoud Ahmadenijad, Osama bin Laden, and many others also shine spotlights on themselves and the tragic period from 2003 to 2009, ensuring that Echoes from Saddam Hussein is a unique and stimulating read.

Contents

2004

2005

2006

2007

2008

2004

CHAPTER 1

Saddam Wears a Beard

I'm still and forevermore President of Iraq and remind you that ninety-nine percent of the people support me. Imagine George W. Bush telling me to get out of my country within forty-eight hours. He's an arrogant little man who considers Iraq a cowboy movie set and himself the gunslinger everyone fears. Really, no one's afraid of Bush the man. In person I'd slap his face and overwhelm him in debate. He needs the American military machine to blow his hot air. Even that didn't frighten me. I remained in Iraq after the criminal invasion of April 2003 and commanded my forces until they disintegrated and still I stayed, eluding bombs, bullets, and barking dogs, and stood defiantly when the infidels found me bearded and unbathed in a hole.

Many laughed and said my fall had been ignominious. On the contrary I felt like a wounded warrior poised for the next offensive. Hundreds of thousands of enemies have fallen under my sword, and I'll soon be free to fight again. My captors are learning their illegal efforts to break me will certainly fail as the international community asks many painful questions. Why was I initially forced into court without an attorney at my side? Why weren't Iraqi reporters allowed to attend? Why was video footage released without sound? Why were tapes later censored and re-released? Can you imagine a power that occupied the United States denying American reporters access to the trial of a former president? All this is unconscionable and why Arabs and others see my trial as a sham and another insult ground into their faces by the world's solitary and ever-righteous superpower.

The Americans are also cowardly in dictating that my trial not be televised either live or on a delayed basis. They fear my charisma and rhetorical ability to attack injustice would galvanize people throughout the Middle East. All Arabs are proud I'm willing to fight our enemies and, when economic catastrophe inevitably overwhelms Iraq, citizens will demand a strong and decisive leader, a man like Stalin, a man like me.

Everyone in Iraq, and surely most in America, realize that Bush and his henchmen are lying that "it's only Al-Qaeda and other foreign elements perpetrating violence in Iraq." Just read the Associated Press report of July ninth, 2004 that quotes U.S. military officials who insist the insurgency is comprised of far more than five thousand men. They either acknowledge that or flunk elementary math. The Americans killed four thousand warriors in April yet still face more enemies every day. Iraqi Sunnis are outraged at losing power and privileges I bestowed them, and forming regional cells led by tribal sheiks who can summon thousands more fighters, assassins, and bomb makers.

It's ominous for Americans that in recent months many of their unnamed officials said insurgents have so much support "they cannot be militarily defeated." That opinion was again reported on July ninth. Does the Bush administration read these reports? We must presume that George W. Bush does not because he hates to read or study or be contradicted. His world, like that of malicious Dick Cheney, is eternally simple: the bad guy is only who America says he is, and he is Saddam. But as the death toll of American soldiers soars, maybe someone else in the administration will concede that many Iraqis are unhappy about the occupation, that they can't be forever repressed, and the solution will have to come through diplomacy. That won't happen without my leadership. Why listen to Bush? He may not hold office much longer. Another Massachusetts blue nose, John Kerry, could be my next opponent.

Moderating the Secret Bush-Kerry Debate

Earlier this week a distinguished Washington, D.C. intelligence operative called to tell me he'd just learned I possessed information that further exposed the hedonistic lifestyles and unrestrained lassitude of the top two presidential candidates. He urged me not to lambaste the leisurely lads online and thereby demolish not merely their current campaigns but their entire political careers. He emphasized that such a sequence would result in Ralph Nader being elected president.

"That's democracy," I said.

"Listen, if you restrain yourself, and let the leading men defend themselves in a secret debate, then you can moderate this historical exchange, which will be televised on pay-per-view before the third official debate."

"What's my take?"

He told me.

"I suppose, then, that it's my patriotic duty."

The agent, intimately connected to both camps, hastily hammered out the terms. Both candidates agreed to be smuggled in gunny sacks out of their current accommodations and flown to an unspecified ICBM silo where they'd meet in the special doom room where two ominous keys, too far apart for even the most long-limbed fellow to simultaneously touch, must be turned at once for strategic activation. Since my real physical identity is unknown, I was able to take a commercial flight to a large Midwest airport but from there was transported in the missile tube of a sleek fighter plane.

As I would offer only my voice and not appear before camera, I did not receive the attention of two gorgeous makeup artists who skillfully, and not without flirtation, prepared the candidates. Kerry opted for his now famous orange makeup and Bush asked for a hardy, soil-of-Midland touch up. After an hour of treatment, both men looked ready to win this war. They were seated by two deferential generals, and cameras ignited.

"Gentlemen, the accusations regarding your lamentable work habits are quite severe," I stated. "I want you to know that I've only taken off three complete days this calendar year."

"Then you're a stupid son-of-a-gun," said Bush.

"My opponent has put it indelicately, but I agree," Kerry said.

"You've both shoved yourselves into the very corner one assumed you'd be trying to evacuate. Very well. I shall direct my first question to President Bush. Sir, the Democrats are saying you're 'lazy' and have an 'aversion to hard work.' Is that true?"

"Certainly not. I've busted more golf balls while in office than any hombre who came before me. And keep in mind, lots of that took place under hot Texas sun."

"It is absolutely typical for my opponent to credit himself for mindless exertion while the real working men and women of this country are blistering their hands in honest endeavor for the meager wages this president wants them to have."

"Listen, Senator," I said. "I have to ask you about your windsurfing, the real details, not superficial attacks by the Republicans. How much time do you really squander blowing around out there?"

"First, I must emphasize, that wind surfing is manifestly more difficult than playing golf on stable land. Skipping across a harsh sea, buffeted by waves, sliced by salty winds, is not man's natural means of movement. It is in fact terribly difficult and always leaves my legs horrifically sore."

"That demonstrates what pitiful condition my opponent is in," Bush said. "How can you expect to defeat the terrorists when you aren't tough enough to get through a sissy sport without moaning?"

"The president is an appalling hypocrite," Kerry responded. "He used to brag about running several miles four times a week. He didn't quit because it was a shameless waste of time. In fact, this president quit jogging because he couldn't take the pain in his knees. Running is man's natural means of travel, yet this man pooped out."

"Senator, when the sun comes up, I challenge you to race me ten kilometers, winner take all."

"You'll not get four more years that way, or any other, Mr. President. If you'd exerted yourself in examining faulty pre-war intelligence reports as much as you did in clearing brush from your ranch, you might not have decided to fight the wrong war in the wrong place at the wrong time."

"You're sending the wrong signals to our troops and to our allies. They'd never follow a gawky guy like you. They know I've led us into the right war in the right place at the right time."

"Gentlemen, please leave politics and foreign policy and all other nonsense out of this debate," I ordered.

"I challenge the president to play me one-on-one in football."

"I'll plant your aching fanny in the sod."

"The game would of course be gentlemanly two-hand touch below the waist."

"Listen, I'm from Texas, and that ain't how we play. What you play ain't football. It's the pansy game the Kennedys played."

"It's disgraceful for a former college cheerleader to impugn America's greatest political family."

"They ain't even the greatest from Massachusetts."

"You just emphasized your Texas roots," I said.

"We're from wherever we want to be from, including Florida, and I'm telling you we're the only family that's had two presidents."

"Hold it," I said. "There was the Adams family."

"Those guys were runts," the president countered. "My dad started at first base for the Yale varsity."

"He may have batted left handed but was no Lou Gehrig," Kerry said.

"Bad-mouth my dad, and I'll kick your butt."

"That's what troubles so many of our friends in the world about this president."

"Senator," I said, "stay on the assigned topics."

"Damn right," said Bush. "Why have you taken off more than sixty days from the campaign trail this year, and thirteen since the convention? While you were windsurfing and touching men's bottoms, I was blowing by you in the polls, and that's a lead I won't be giving up."

"Mr. President, I was working on my days away from the campaign. What were you achieving for the country the forty percent of the time during your presidency you've either been down on the ranch or sailing at Kennebunkport or hiding in Camp David? That's a rhetorical question, of course. We already know none of your activities has benefited the American people in time of war."

"This opponent is like so many liberals. He thinks he knows what other people are doing and exactly how they're thinking. I guarantee you, I've got offices at all those places and work hard when I'm there. I work even harder there than at the White House because there're fewer distractions.

"I also want to point out that Senator Kerry is a kept man. His wife's got about a billion bucks, and he doesn't know anything about the real men and women of this country."

"Mr. President, that is a despicable cheap shot. My wife and I may be immersed in luxury, but it's not our fault. She inherited the money from her first husband, Senator Heinz, a Republican. Her patrimony is our burden."

"It's your ticket. You're an inept senator and couldn't have made a living in the world of honest business."

"Balderdash. In fact, no wildcatter ever drilled more dry holes than you."

"At least I didn't have to tug my wife's skirt for money."

"Mr. President, I'm an oft-wounded veteran of war, and not all of my wounds were self-inflicted. If you again insult my wife or my marriage, I'll use combat techniques to kick your gluteus maximus."

Both men sprang from their thrones.

"All right boys," I shouted, "let's get it on. But stay away from those damn keys."

Translating Bush and Kerry in the Final Debate

"I'd like to welcome President Bush and Senator Kerry to our third and final debate," said the moderator. "And I shall remind the audience to at all times maintain silence. Anyone audibly displaying emotion will be evicted by force.

"My first question is for Senator Kerry. Sir, do you think our children will ever live in a world as safe as the one in which we grew up?"

"What safe world was that? The world of the Great Depression, of World War II, of the Korean War and the debacle in Vietnam? Are you referring to the civil rights battles of the Fifties and Sixties as being safe? We have in fact always lived in a wretched and dangerous world, but we can indeed become safer, and the only way to do that is to remove George W. Bush from the White House. This arrogant and intemperate man rushed us into a war we did not need to fight and he did so with inadequate numbers of troops to maintain peace – as his envoy in Iraq, J. Paul Bremer, recently and quite publicly noted. Furthermore, at our nation's ports the president is permitting ninety-five percent of the containers to enter without being examined. Why isn't he himself down there peering into those containers?"

"I'm prepared to personally examine as many containers as I can, though I don't think I should allocate more than five hours of my day to this task. I know damn well I could examine more containers per hour than John Kerry, a guy who'd be too busy lecturing his servants how to polish crystal and silver.

"My opponent doesn't understand that we can only be strong if we stay on the offensive and hold countries accountable if they harbor terrorists. I have a comprehensive plan, a manly plan. And what does my opponent have: the pitiful idea that terrorism is only a nuisance, like prostitution. This guy, if elected president – which many times a day I fall to my knees and pray he won't be – could very well get us all killed."

"President Bush," said the moderator, "how could we have had such a shortage of flu vaccines? We're a nation of vast wealth."

"Some two-bit company in England didn't produce anywhere near

9

the number of vaccines they'd promised and we'd depended on. I'd liked to have booted some tail."

"That underscores the president's lack of vision," said Kerry. "More than five million vulnerable human beings have lost health care coverage on his watch. We now have forty-five million uninsured, a million of them right here in what would otherwise be your desert paradise of Arizona. I have a plan that would give every man, woman, and child in this nation the same superb health care we enjoy in the United States Senate."

"A litany of complaints is not a plan," said the president. "What he's talking about would cost the nation five trillion dollars. He makes empty promises, standing there like a giraffe from Massachusetts."

"Senator Kerry," said the moderator, "how can you achieve your goals if you keep your pledge not to raise taxes on those who make less than two hundred thousand dollars a year?"

"I would restore fiscal discipline. I would tighten belts. I would pull the straps of girdles and corsets. I believe in the pay-as-you-go approach."

"Isn't that ridiculous?" said the president. "This liberal voted ninety-eight times to raise taxes. His rhetoric doesn't match his record. Let's not forget that Ted Kennedy is the conservative senator from Massachusetts."

"Our oil-splotched president – that being other people's oil since he never found any when he was in the business – didn't do his homework. If he had, he'd know that I've voted for tax cuts more than six hundred times."

"Mr. President," said the moderator, "what can we do about the divisive issue of gay marriage?"

"The first thing we do is emphasize that most gays are Democrats, probably about ninety-five percent of them. But I do believe respect is important, and my public position is that I respect them. I just don't like bad lifestyle choices of either a political or sexual nature."

"For decades I have talked to many gay people – though I've never had any of their urges – and I know that being gay is not a choice. Gay people are born that way, and I respect that. I respect Dick Cheney's daughter, and future Vice President John Edwards and I often profess our admiration for that young lady. She didn't choose to be gay any more than she chose to be the daughter of Machiavelli."

"Senator Kerry, you're a Catholic," said the moderator. "Your church says it's wrong to support abortions, yet you support abortions. How do you reconcile that?"

"I am a very religious man. We are all God's children and He determines everything. I'm proud to again tell the nation that I was a devout altar boy. And no, I was not molested. Those men in robes, despite their powerful inherent urges, would never have tried anything perverse with a future warrior. At any rate, I passionately believe in a woman's right to make this most personal of decisions. In Roe v. Wade the Supreme Court vowed to stay out of the bedrooms and abortion clinics. It's clear that this president is trying to appoint justices who will overturn Roe v. Wade."

"Is that true, Mr. President?"

"I believe in good laws to reduce the number of abortions and promote the culture of life. Adoption, maternity group homes, and abstinence are wonderful alternatives."

"He didn't answer the question," said Kerry.

"I did so. And I challenge Democrats to practice more abstinence."

"In that case, Mr. President, I challenge you to vow you'll abstain for the next four years."

"I'm prepared to make that pledge if you'll do the same."

"I so pledge."

From the audience their respective wives gasped.

"President Bush," the moderator said, "our social security system is in deep doo doo. What do you think we should do?"

"We should take lots of that money out of the social security system. That means take it out of the government's hands and invest it in individual accounts. I know a lot of wealthy folks our citizens could hire to make that money grow."

"That would be a disaster, a two trillion dollar hole," said Kerry. "Today's workers pay for today's retirees. We must not privatize social security or cut benefits. I certainly wouldn't. It's elementary. This president's tax cut for the wealthiest one percent of the population would have saved social security for another seventy years."

Laughing, the president said, "I don't know where my opponent gets those numbers, probably from some drug-crazed hippie living on the streets of San Francisco. I'll tell you another thing we should do: ask the senator's wife to donate her unearned fortune to the social security system. That would save it for quite a spell. I'm also prepared to order my wife to turn over her personal fortune to social security."

"That's mathematically inequitable."

"But ethically equal."

"This president's hostility toward women is further underscored by his denying a decent minimum wage to nine million mothers who are struggling to raise children. If he had simply raised the minimum from about five dollars an hour to seven, each of these poor women would have earned almost four thousand dollars more. But this president instead preferred to give a hundred-thousand-dollar-plus tax break to his millionaire friends. I'm tired of his talk of family values while he creates conditions that make it impossible for millions of families to flourish."

"I again say to you Democrats, particularly the majority who have loose morals and are undereducated, go back to school. Learn a trade. Learn a profession. It's time for you ignoramuses to get a real education. Quit producing more children than you can take care of, and start maintaining morality and discipline in your homes. Don't you have the sense to make your kids behave at school?"

"Senator Kerry, what do you think we can do about the immigration crisis?" said the moderator.

"The borders are leaking more now than before 9/11. We also need to enforce the laws against hiring illegal aliens."

"It ridiculous for my opponent to deny that we're much better protected today with me in charge. Remember, I was the governor of a border state, and a real big one. I know all about protecting borders. As president I've put a thousand more agents to work, and they're armed with a lot of neat high-tech equipment. And if necessary, I'll go down and personally patrol the border. It's not that far from my ranch. Senator Kerry, even with his wife's fleet of jets, probably couldn't make it there from Massachusetts."

"I could most certainly report for border duty, Mr. President. And far more regularly than you showed up for your National Guard commitments. I know about duty. I'm in fact at this moment ready to wince because of the recurring agony of my war wounds."

"Senator Kerry, what is your position about reinstituting the draft?"

"I'm not only against the draft, I'm against this president's back door draft that first recalls reservists then holds them for periods far longer than even my tour of duty in Vietnam."

"That's been the only way to protect my dear friends, the Iraqis. Now the best way to take pressure off them is to train them to be great warriors. We'll soon have a hundred twenty-five thousand of them."

"I suggest you join them in combat, Mr. President."

"I will, if you're by my side."

"While we're alluding to firepower, I'd like to ask the president what he thinks about legal assault weapons," said the moderator.

"The best way to serve America is to prosecute the criminals. Assault weapons don't kill people. People kill people. And we need to kill the people who're killing people."

"I'm a hunter and I'm a gun owner," said Senator Kerry. "In my lifetime I have doubtless killed far more people and animals than this preppy president. I also used to run one of the largest and toughest district attorneys offices in the country. I know about prosecuting. I've put countless people behind bars. I also know about the real world. If the president lived there, he'd know that the police are often outgunned by criminals armed with assault weapons. That's why most law enforcement agencies wanted a ban on assault weapons. Instead, this president kowtowed to the National Rifle Association."

"I did not. And I want to emphasize that I'm ready to ensure our police always have the advantage in firepower. I'm willing to arm every officer in this nation with a bazooka and make sure every police department has plenty of tanks. That's the price we must pay to maintain law and order and to ensure that no American ever has to live without a personal assault weapon."

The audience erupted, some gasping, others cheering.

"Quiet, or I'll have this building cleared," said the moderator. "President Bush, what part does your faith play in your decision making?"

"It plays a real big part. I pray for the troops. I pray for my family and my little girls. I pray for guidance. I can do His work because prayer has given me calmness in the storm."

"I respect that, and am confident that I pray even more than the president, who was never an altar boy. But I believe that decisions should be based on earthly considerations, and only after open consultation with our allies around the world."

"What you're really saying is that you want retreat and defeat in Iraq."

"I didn't say or imply that."

"That's what your policies would lead to."

"That's speculation. What is fact is that your policies have made America countless enemies it didn't have before you attacked Iraq."

"Our country had been attacked."

"Not by Iraq."

"Terrorists were everywhere."

"Not in Iraq."

"You'd be soft on terrorism."

"Nonsense. I plan to kill every one of them, and more than a few I'd personally eliminate in hand-to-hand combat."

"For all you know, I've already done the same."

"I doubt it."

"Gentlemen," said the moderator, "stop this conversation at once. It's against the rules."

"I don't think my opponent wants the Iraqi people to be free," said the president.

"I certainly do."

"Yet you would've permitted Saddam Hussein to remain in power."

"We had him weakened and contained, and United Nations officials were on the ground, verifying what we've learned and relearned: Iraq had no weapons of mass destruction."

"Then why did you vote in the Senate to authorize force?"

"You misled me."

"I was looking at the same intelligence reports you were."

"Nonsense. You were privy to more misinformation."

"You think it's politically beneficial to change positions, so that's what you've done – change positions."

"Gentlemen, I'm sorry but I'm going to have to shut you both up."

"You can't shut me up. I'm not only the president but I'm speaking for God, who every day tells me I'm his instrument of liberation here on earth."

"That's not what He tells me," said the senator.

"God may listen to you, but He doesn't talk to you. He wouldn't waste time on a flip-flopper who lacks core convictions."

"What an outrageous and self-serving statement."

"That's the problem with Democrats. You still can't accept that God is on our side."

Kerry Hunts for Macho Voters in Ohio

"Howdy, I'd like to buy me a huntin' licence," said John Kerry.

"What kind?" said the ruddy-face store owner.

"Don't matter. I love killin' anything that walks or flies."

"What about fish?"

"Gut those babies with my teeth."

"Right now, it's geese season."

"Okay, partner," said Kerry. "I reckon that'll do."

"You from around these parts?" said the Ohioan.

"Pretty much. Massachusetts."

"Massachusetts?"

"Yeah, northern, cold, and tough, just like this territory."

"Okay, here you are."

"God bless you and all the decent folks around here."

John Kerry, standing tall as John Wayne, shoved the license into a pocket of his glistening new camouflage hunting uniform. Then, followed by a phalanx of photographers and reporters, he was driven to a very fine kill zone. The media people had to stay back. It might be dangerous. Kerry, a decorated and oft-wounded war veteran, and three comrades, presumably also bearing wounds and decorations, would stalk the geese alone.

While on patrol, Kerry and his men could sometimes be seen. Often, though, there was only silence from a seemingly empty field. Occasionally, the media people heard gunfire. A few minutes after one volley, Kerry was spotted as he picked up something next to a distant tree. A reporter with a zoom lens snapped a photo. Sure enough, the senator had killed a goose – at least someone had – and his right hand was bloody from picking up the trophy.

When the four hunters returned, the photographers shouted, "Senator, can we get a shot of your right hand. Senator, please."

Kerry, right hand immersed in his sleeve, waved them off with his left.

"Senator, I'm no reporter. I'm a legendary Ohio hunter, and I'd like to know why you aren't carrying your own kill. That's what a real man does."

"I don't have a bird bag."

"A true hunter never goes out without his bird bag."

"What if he's huntin' deer," Kerry said.

"Did you clean that bird yourself?"

"We haven't cleaned any of 'em yet."

"An honorable hunter always cleans his own game."

"I guarantee you I'll clean my own goose and my buddies' geese too."

"That would dishonor them," said the hunter. "And that's not all, Senator. How in the hell did you get to hunt on this premium land? Most of us would kill to hunt in a place like this."

"Close personal friends invited me," said the senator.

"Who are they?" shouted a reporter.

Kerry stroked his chin with his shiny left hand, glanced at an aide, who glanced at another aide. "We gotta respect their privacy," said tall John.

That night at a political rally, John Kerry came under fire.

"Senator," a journalist reported, "at a speech this afternoon Vice President Cheney said, 'My fellow sportsmen, don't be fooled. John Kerry's new camouflage jacket is an October surprise to disguise the fact that he votes against gun owner rights every time.'"

"That's horse hooey. I love guns. I just recently went skeet shooting, and I went hunting earlier this year in Iowa before the caucuses. The citizens there damn sure saw a straight-shooter."

"Senator," said another journalist, "a representative of the National Rifle Association has just said you're 'no friend' of sports shooters."

"What's he talkin' about? I'll bet he wasn't out huntin' today."

"He's referring to your desire to ban assault rifles."

"A real marksman doesn't need fancy weapons to shoot geese. Only noncombatant slackers like the incumbents need guns like that. Those guys and the criminals, of course."

"Many Republicans have characterized your hunting trip as a transparent political ploy," said a TV newswoman. "What's your response?"

"I began huntin' at age twelve, the same time I became an altar boy. My early training, and the fact I always carried my rosary, convinced

God to save me during countless firefights in Viet Nam. I guarantee you, I'll always love guns. And I'm against gay marriage, too."

"Senator, what's your response to the president's comment today?"

"What did that tinhorn say?"

"The president said, 'He can run, even in a cam suit, but he can't hide.'"

"Not only am I not hidin', I promise right here that next week I'm gonna go huntin' on the president's ranch, and I'm gonna shoot as many animals as possible, including dogs and cats."

"What if the president tries to stop you?" said a reporter.

"Let him try."

"Senator, can we please talk about politics?" asked a man from a national magazine.

"Sure, but only for a short spell."

"The Republican Party in Ohio has hired and trained almost four thousand recruits to challenge voters at the polls. They can ask a poll worker to question anyone who doesn't look like a citizen, or who doesn't appear to be at least eighteen, or who doesn't look like a resident, or who seems like he hasn't lived in Ohio for thirty days."

"We all know the Republicans want to limit the number of people who vote. They'll try to create long lines and force some people to go away. Don't worry, though. The Democrats'll have two thousand recruits there to protect legitimate voters."

"Your recruits will still be outnumbered two to one in a state that could very well decide the election."

"No big deal," said the Senator. "After doin' my patriotic duty in Massachusetts, I'll jet to Ohio in my cam suit, and armed with an assault rifle – only for that occasion – I'll personally patrol dozens of voting booths."

"Are you worried Arnold Schwarzenegger will be campaigning here the weekend before Election Day?"

"Not a whit. That'll just give me a chance to beat his butt before he runs against me in 2008."

Experimental Poll

Arturo Ali swore he hadn't intended to further polarize a nation already overwrought by war, gaping deficits, inflammatory debates, repetitive stump speeches, self-righteous attacks by campaign staffs, and especially by talk radio hosts who could not be avoided since fanatical followers used their places of business as launch pads for ear-splitting drivel. Indeed, no man had a greater desire to lessen the agony of his adopted country than Arturo Ali.

He'd come to the United States in the trunk of a car at age five, cradled by his African-Arab father and Mexican mother as they crossed the border at Tijuana. His father soon tired of toiling in a series of Los Angeles sweat shops and returned to Yemen, promising to send money and someday return. He did neither, and Ali and his mother moved in with a dozen of her relatives in a two bedroom apartment in East L.A. After only a year of schooling, he became fluent in English and compiled a 4.35 (out of a possible 4) grade point average from second grade through high school graduation. He had no interest in attending famous universities far away or even on the other side of town. He studied at Cal State Los Angeles and got a teaching credential so he could help new residents of this nation become proud and productive citizens. For Arturo Ali, the commitment was clear: he would teach English as a Second Language for adults, a group that had to produce rapidly or face deportation or starvation or both.

"You not only have an obligation to learn English and work hard, you must read about and discuss the issues of the day," Ali frequently told his students. "And then you must vote."

"But we aren't citizens yet," his students would respond.

"Be patient. That day will come."

Last Friday, Arturo Ali faced his class, smiled with even greater than customary vigor, marched to the door, opened it, and said, "Ladies and gentlemen, with pride and amazement, I'd like to introduce you to Walter Cronkite."

The students stared at the camera and cameraman and were silent except for a man who said: "Quíen es el viejo?" (Who's the old man?)

Ali clinched fists at his sides before saying, "Thank you for coming, Mr. Cronkite. You don't speak Spanish, do you?"

"No sir, I don't."

"Good. I mean, it's better you can't so you'll have to speak English.

"Class, I can't believe he's already been off the air for a generation – this is Walter Cronkite, the most famous TV newscaster in history."

Now there was strong applause and faces brightened in the glare of just-perceived celebrity. Cronkite devoted a few minutes to highlights of his career as the most trusted man in the free world. Then he focused on the reason for his visit: "Your teacher is one of the finest Americans I've ever met. He's dedicated his life to giving you the skills to uphold your most important obligation in a democratic society: that is to vote. And that's just what we're going to do here today."

Arturo Ali had already cut up a handful of blank strips of paper, and he passed out one to each of 38 students in attendance.

"All right," said Cronkite, "cast your presidential ballot."

"Do we write our names on the papers?" a lady asked.

"No," said Ali.

"You always tell us to write our names," she said.

"You have complete privacy in the voting booth," Cronkite assured her.

In less than five minutes all the ballots had been written on and passed in, and Cronkite himself, soothed by the camera, sat at Ali's desk and counted the votes. He then signed his name to the tally sheet, stood and declared: "It's official. Thirty-six of you voted for John Kerry and two for George W. Bush. And that's the way it is on October 29, 2004."

Cronkite's declaration was the lead story on every newscast in the land, and stations were immediately inundated with calls either laudatory or hysterical.

Four samples follow:

"Walter Cronkite is still a great American and defender of all Americans, even those who aren't yet citizens."

"If that pinko geezer isn't put away, it's a national travesty."

"It's touching that a man so renowned cares about those so small."

"The Supreme Court should intervene if W loses this election because

of Cronkite's propaganda and the illegal voting."

That final comment first horrified and then galvanized the Republican Party, which had already mobilized thousands of paid, trained, and supremely-motivated poll watchers. And this army of Praetorian Guards for democracy quintupled in size over the weekend. On Election Day – November 2, 2004 – they were out with attitude, and many were rumored to be armed with assault weapons. The Democratic poll watchers reportedly countered with copies of The Constitution tucked in their pockets and purses.

Television crews had for three days been encamped outside Ali's house of barred windows about 10 miles southeast of downtown Los Angeles. He'd called in sick Monday, his first absence in a decade, and Tuesday morning he stepped outside and declared, "I urge you to focus on the issues. Leave me alone."

"When will you be voting?" asked a female reporter, microphone in hand.

"None of your business."

"Afraid?"

"Not at all."

Ali walked back inside and called the school with news of continuing illness.

Conditions were far tenser at polling places in many states that, unlike California, were undecided. In Miami three men speaking Spanish approached the polls.

"Look at them," a watcher said to a worker.

"What?"

"They aren't citizens. They can't even speak English."

"Gentlemen," said the worker. "May I please speak to you?"

"Sí," they said.

"Are you U.S. citizens?"

"No, we're Chinese," the youngest said.

"Let me see your passports," said the watcher.

"Let me see yours," said another man.

"Prove your U.S. citizens."

"You prove you're a citizen," said the youngest.

"I don't have to. Listen to me. I don't have an accent."

"Yeah, you do. You've got the accent of a redneck."

"I'm challenging all three of these men," said the watcher. "If this election goes to the Supreme Court again, I'll make sure they're checked out, along with hundreds of others I've seen today."

In inner-city Milwaukee, a young black man strode toward the booth.

"Just a minute," said a Red-State poll watcher. "How old are you?"

"A lot younger than you."

"Sir," said an official, nonpartisan poll worker. "You're not to harass the voters. You're to inform us if you have doubts."

"Okay, I so inform you."

"Of what?" she said.

"I don't think this guy's eighteen."

"Young man, may I please see your driver's license?" said the poll worker.

He handed it to her.

"He's twenty," she said.

"Maybe so, but we really need one of those special lights to check for fake ID's."

In Cleveland, two black women were arm in arm approaching the polling place.

"You two can't marry, you know," said the poll watcher.

"We're sisters."

"You from around here?"

They ignored him and walked on. He ran to a poll worker who accompanied him toward the women about to enter adjacent booths.

"Just a minute, please," said the worker. "This official watcher doesn't think you look like residents of Cleveland."

"What's a resident of Cleveland look like?"

"Show us some ID," said the watcher.

Both ladies handed their licenses to the worker.

"They both have Cleveland addresses."

"I'm amazed," said the watcher. "We sent out tens of thousands of letters to Democrats in this area and about a third came back either undeliverable or with names like Mary Poppins."

"Must be a communist conspiracy," said the previously-silent sister.

In Las Vegas a burly black man wearing dusty clothes approached the place of ultimate polls.

"Hold it right there, buster," said a watcher.

"What's the problem?" said a vigilant worker.

"This guy looks like he just got to town, hiking through the desert."

"Listen, four-eyes, I just got off my construction job."

"You don't look like a local resident. Must've cashed the welfare check and come to Vegas to gamble."

"Bleep you."

"Then you probably blew all your money and have been sleeping in the streets."

"That's intolerable language," said the worker. "I'm sure this gentleman has ID, don't you, sir?"

He handed her a piece of paper.

"What's that?" said the watcher.

"A temporary license," said the worker.

"He has to have been here the minimum number of days."

"Let's see. He's had this license two days more than that."

"You liberals," said the watcher.

Arturo Ali watched many similar confrontations all day on TV. That night, shortly after each candidate gave a victory speech and their parties demanded judicial intervention, he stepped into his garage and jabbed the brakes as he backed through cameras. In big L.A. traffic had lessened and was now only thick instead of gridlocked. Crawling toward the freeway, Ali blew his horn at the driver in front, trying to prod him to merge more aggressively, then was honked at by a driver who hadn't wanted to let either in. This familiar sequence relaxed Ali and he enjoyed the drive. But cameras were waiting at the polling place.

"Arturo Ali?" said a U.S. Marshal, surrounded by poll watchers.

"Yes, sir."

"We have documentation that your mother used fraudulent documents to obtain her U.S. citizenship and therefore was an invalid sponsor for your citizenship. You're an alien, Mr. Ali, and I hereby place you under arrest."

What President Bush Really Said

Armed with a pocket-size and still top secret mind-reading device just developed by alarmed and bitter liberal scientists, this reporter attended President George W. Bush's recent macho victory speech. It was a stirring event. The president looked tanned, rested, physically fit, sartorially sharp, and most of all he looked proud and happy. He had a right to be ecstatic. Only two score and three men in this nation's history have been elected president, and but a fraction of those have done so twice. Let's be gracious and concede that in George W. Bush we're talking about a political powerhouse perhaps rivaling Richard M. Nixon. True, President Bush's mandate wasn't nearly as overwhelming as President Nixon's in 1972 but both incumbents clobbered anti-war weaklings and made arrogance sexy.

Humbling the lectern with two strong hands, President Bush started speaking but we heard something else: "Four years ago I came to this bureaucratic hick town with an overwhelming mandate from millions of angry Americans who didn't care the other guy got a half-million more votes. Imagine what I'm going to do now with fifty-one percent of the people behind me. I'm not merely going to spend my political capital, I'm going jam it down your throats. That's my style. I didn't come here to just say I served. I'm here to make big-time changes.

"Look what I've already achieved. Let's start with the federal budget. I inherited a big surplus. Now we've got a deficit of almost three trillion. My tax cuts and foreign aggression were the key factors, and I aim to make them permanent. We also had a net loss of jobs during my first term. Unemployment is on the march. I thank my architect, Karl Rove, for that literary nugget. He understands that people without jobs must borrow money from the haves and have-mores who comprise my base."

"Just a minute, Mr. President," a reporter interjected. "It was hard-working evangelicals of middle America who got you elected."

"I didn't call on you, so keep your mouth shut or you'll be outta here fast as hecklers at my campaign revival speeches. And that reminds me. From now on, there'll be no complicated questions that are really two questions and there'll be no follow up questions. Only one question apiece, and only after I address you by your last name, like Bear Bryant would've done.

"Returning to the economic front, we have my social security plan, which, believe me, you're going to adopt. We'll slash that antiquated program for working stiffs by a quarter or a third, and we'll put that money in private investments, stocks and things like that."

"Mr. President," another reporter shouted, "many economists say that would bankrupt an already strained system."

Like an aggrieved umpire, the president thrust a finger at the exit, and several secret agents carried her head first out the door.

The president shook his head, straightened his tie, reattached himself to the lectern, and said, "We're going to smash terrorism and, frankly, anything that may be nearby. That's how it must be. Our effeminate non-allies in Europe can't be counted on, so it will be our blood and money that get it done whether or not it needs doing.

"Elections are coming right up in Iraq. They'll go well because I'm going to annihilate the insurgents in Fallujah. After that I'll decide whether to use my capital to attack Iran or North Korea."

"But Mr. President," said a White House correspondent. "Iran is more than twice as large as Texas and has more than twice as many people as Iraq. And North Korea is probably already nuclear armed and can anyway easily flatten Seoul by conventional means."

"Get him outta here," said the president.

As the correspondent was being hauled away, another journalist said, "Mr. President, we might have a thousand casualties a week against a powerful army like North Korea's."

"Yeah, but we'd kill more of them."

"The American people aren't going to put up with that."

"If I ultimately conclude that, then I'll mark Syria as the ultimate terrorist threat. Now get his ass outta here."

2005

CHAPTER 2

What Bush Could Be Thinking about Iraq

Okay, I deceived you – and myself, too, I guess – to get us into Iraq. But that doesn't matter anymore. People are giving me a pass. We're at war. More than ten thousand Americans have been wounded in combat and more than a thousand died. That means nine out of ten wounded are surviving. That's an extraordinary testament to our helmets and vests which often save the body but, unfortunately, not the arms and legs and face. We'll probably have an even higher rate of survival now that we've received some reporter-planted complaints from soldiers and had to speed up armoring vehicles. I also have to thank our doctors who save lives by instantly operating in combat zones. Our pilots and airplanes are great too. They can get the most severely wounded warriors back to the United States in four days. During the Viet Nam War that took six weeks; and only one in four wounded survived the communists, who were planning to conquer us.

Now we've got a lot to be thankful for. Those civilian casualties the liberal media have been telling you about aren't ours. I'm also sure the reports are exaggerated, those claiming that the United States has killed ten thousand Iraqi civilians. And those estimates of fifteen or twenty thousand dead are way off. We pride ourselves on limiting collateral damage. And I guess I'm lucky I don't spend much time thinking about how many Iraqis we've mangled. There's no way their medical care is as good as ours, so I'll bet no more than three-quarters of their casualties survive. So let's say we've wounded or maimed sixty thousand Iraqi noncombatants, at most. It's unfortunate, but we've got to do this or sure as hell it'll soon be happening in Omaha.

I'd like to call our enemies in Iraq terrorists but you know the word everyone insists on using – insurgents. They really are a primitive bunch, cutting off people's heads, planting roadside bombs, and trying to force people to be as backward as they are. They're the worst. But there aren't that many of them. That's what I believe anyway, and hope you do too. I'd frequently been told, and then told you, there were only a handful of foreign terrorists. Then last spring I heard there were as many as three thousand insurgents, most from Iraq. And we quickly

29

killed at least three thousand of them. But up popped reports they then numbered five thousand or more. I can't figure that out. I know the liberal media is lying about my policies creating more enemies. Anyway, we soon killed ten thousand or more of them. So what do I read this week? Hell, now there are twelve, eighteen, even twenty thousand insurgents. I'm not going to admit it, but it looks like every time we kill one, two take his place.

As bad as I've screwed things up, there really is a chance that something wonderful will happen. Late next month, as you know, there will be democratic elections for the first time in the several thousand year history of Iraq. Damn, that means Iraq is even older than the world so many of my followers and I believe in. Anyway, the Iraqi people will have a chance at liberty. I can't imagine they don't want it. I'm just concerned, very privately, that they don't want it badly enough. They don't seem to want freedom as badly as the insurgents want repression. That's what it looks like, doesn't it? All the time I get these reports of ten, twenty, or thirty Iraqi police officers being slaughtered while on duty in their jail. Or sometimes they're marched out front and shot in the head. It's about the same with Iraqi soldiers. They're often ambushed. Awhile back that sure was embarrassing when we'd just trained fifty soldiers then sent them home unarmed riding a bus, and all of them were forced onto the ground and murdered. How do you explain those wartime soldiers being unarmed? More importantly today – do Iraqi police or soldiers ever kill any insurgents?

Don't tell me you wouldn't have screwed up too if you'd tried to run a war like this, or any other. The bottom line is if the Iraqi people want democracy, we've given them the opportunity to have it. If they can't defend themselves against the insurgents – aided by our soldiers, arms, and money – then they don't want what we're offering.

Surgically Enhanced Saddam

I am a different man. I am a new and much better man. I have never felt so grateful, though of course I would not have voluntarily had the operation. My captors stormed into my cell and like a warrior I fought them. I struck and kicked and cursed and called them scoundrels and dogs and worse. They were attacking the rightful President of Iraq and, more than besmirching my authority, they were degrading me in the most vile and personal ways. I threatened them with an eternity of suffering. I promised to inflict much of it myself. And that is my final memory until wakening with an unimaginable headache.

Thankfully, the pain daily eased, and early in my recovery I was placed on a regimen of tranquilizers that, in concert with surgery, began to give me a calm and clear state of mind I'd simply never had. Doctors then diligently explained that I'd undergone a novel lobotomy-like adjustment to the front of my brain, a mysterious region known to swarm with violent and obsessive impulses. Thrice weekly private consultations have also been enormously helpful, giving me the opportunity to discuss – and in part exorcise – the childhood beatings I received, as well as the countless acts of cruelty I've visited on humanity. My daily group therapy sessions were at first quite difficult since my fellow prisoners tried, it seemed, to impale me with all responsibility for evil deeds. Without attempting to mitigate my guilt, I did politely yet forcefully tell these gentlemen they too were responsible for their acts, and not always correct in asserting I would have killed them if they'd declined to commit crimes I ordered.

No doubt, however, I alone am responsible for a lifetime of being Saddam, and now at last, in the final fifteen years of so of my journey, I am equipped to be something better, something unlike any of you would have expected. I stand here in my claustrophobic cell, in such contrast to the mighty dictator who reigned from so many palaces, and through this radio microphone I tell you I have seen the future, and it is democracy – the mandate of history. In confirmation we must inevitably note that tyranny has foredoomed hundreds of thousands of us to death or mutilation on battlefields of otherwise dubious significance. It has also poisoned the lives of countless terrorized and tortured citizens, and caused us, rightly or not, to be invaded and occupied by a powerful military force. Though the alien presence is undeniably painful, it will end when security and self-determination are at least in healthy infancy.

I tell you, my brave and earnest Iraqi people, that you deserve a better government and a better life. Greatness lies within you. I do not ask you to forgive me for so long suppressing your gifts. Rather, I urge you to exercise your inherent talent. I have unqualified confidence in your integrity and vigor. January thirtieth will soon be at hand. Protect your rights. Embrace this day. Cherish the opportunity to express your will. Vow this Election Day is the first in a permanent procession. I shall be thinking of you. I shall be with you, awaiting your achievement of the peace and happiness I was unable to provide but will nevertheless, from my humble cell, forever share with all free Iraqis."

The producer turned off the microphone and embraced me. "Magnificent."

"Did I sound like Saddam?"

"Absolutely, you're the best Saddam we've ever had."

Dashing Saddam Deluged by Proposals

Ignore reports that Saddam Hussein is planning to sue those responsible for publishing a photo of him wearing luminous white underwear as he stood washing clothes in his prison cell. Saddam did initially demand that his legal team file a five billion dollar suit against infidels presuming to snoop on and publicly degrade the man who still considers himself the eternal President of Iraq. His attorneys had to persuade their client to desist, however, after he was buried by more than a hundred thousand letters from enchanted women around the world. That's hardly grounds for proving one's soul has been grievously assaulted.

Saddam was further mollified when informed his love-letter tally topped the combined total received by Charles Manson, Ted Bundy, and Scott Peterson. And, most encouragingly, a majority of the women enclosed photos of themselves wearing substantially less than cover-boy Saddam. Studying the alluring shots perked Saddam up but, alas, his petition for a hundred conjugal visits a month was denied. The tyrant said okay once a month. That too was nixed. His adroit attorneys were at least able to win for Saddam the right to retain as many letters and photos as he can squeeze into his cell, and to post on the walls up to a dozen images at a time.

That final legal maneuver was only reluctantly undertaken by Saddam's legal experts since they'd prefer he study indictments for mass murder and examine photos of corpses and skeletons. The illustrious defendant demurred. And one surely can understand his reading preferences. Photocopies of some letters were smuggled to us by a now-wealthy attorney. Excerpts follow.

Dear Saddam,

I've always thought you were very handsome and charismatic, and was sad when you were captured looking so dirty and scruffy and scared. I thought you'd never regain that magical masculinity, but you have. You look terrific. You've lost most of that paunch you had when you were in power, and very few guys sixty-eight years old have such wonderful thick black hair. I'm going to be vacationing in Baghdad this summer and will do everything possible to visit you.

P.S. – My photo was just taken last week. And, yes, they're real.

Susie in Shreveport

Dear Saddam,

I'm going to tell you what's in my heart. I want to bear your child. In fact, I want to have several of your children. This would also be great for you since you need a male heir after the terrible loss of your two boys last year. I also want you to know that every guy I've been out with tells me I'm a very passionate and sensuous woman. I doubt that will shock you since you don't seem all that religious. And, besides, I know lots of your girlfriends weren't virgins when you first summoned them.

Please tell me you're interested and I'll rent a place in Baghdad so I can be close to you. You're near Baghdad, aren't you? I hope they don't have you down at Guantanamo Bay. I'm sure they don't or you wouldn't look so cute.

Magda in Munich

Dear Saddam,

You have forever been my favorite dictator and are obviously much bigger and manlier than Kim Jong-il, whom I personally work for in a confidential capacity. I'm tired of him. I'm tired of North Korea. It is as dreary as our dictator. I want to be with a colorful man in an exciting place. I want to be with you. I can help you with your defense. I know you'd win with my loving support. Then you can resurrect your political career. You have all the personal qualities necessary to win a real election. You can again be President, and I'll join you as the First Lady of Iraq.

Pam in Pyongyang

Dear Saddam,

Please forgive me for my bold advance but it is the only way to capture your attention. I have it now, don't I? I'm sure I do. You've always been a renowned lady's man. Now you need a special woman. You need me. And I want you. You can't imagine how much. I'm right here, too. I know where they're keeping you. I'm friends with some authorities. They also admire you and have promised to help me see you if you consent. Please say yes. I know you must be lonely. Once I visit, that will never be a problem.

Faribi in Baghdad

News Bulletin – Less than two weeks after publication of his sensational photo, Saddam Hussein was visited in his cell. Faribi entered wearing an elegant ivory evening gown and asked the guards to grant some privacy. They complied and did not interrupt despite hearing moans of evident mutual ecstasy. After two hours, the guards were obliged to return. They saw Faribi standing barefoot in her ivory evening gown. At her toes lay Saddam, his underwear reddening around a knife.

"Don't worry," she said. "He didn't suffer like my father."

President Bush Warns of More Destruction

Last week, stern and righteous, I looked into the teleprompter and pronounced: "Tonight I want to discuss a grave threat to peace; the threat comes from Iraq. It arises from the Iraqi drive toward an arsenal of terror. We're concerned about the link between Iraq developing weapons of terror, and the wider war on terror. The threat from Iraq stands alone because of its past and present actions, its technological capabilities, and the merciless nature of its regime. Saddam Hussein is a homicidal dictator addicted to weapons of mass destruction."

I pointed a hard index finger at Karl Rove's head, and that meant to quit jumping and waving his arms at me. Then I continued.

"We know that Saddam's regime has produced thousands of tons of chemical agents, including mustard gas and nerve gas. And surveillance photos reveal the regime is rebuilding facilities it had used to produce chemical and biological weapons. Saddam Hussein has chosen to build and keep these weapons despite international sanctions, U.N. demands, and isolation from the civilized world."

Dick Cheney started leaping even higher than Rove so I stopped speaking and ground my teeth until he sat down.

"We are also urgently concerned about Saddam's links to international terrorist groups. We know that Iraq and Al Qaeda share a common enemy – the United States. We know that Iraq and Al Qaeda have had high-level contact for a decade. Some Al Qaeda leaders fled from Afghanistan to Iraq. One very senior Al Qaeda leader received medical treatment in Baghdad this year. We've also learned that Iraq has trained Al Qaeda members in bomb-making and poisons and deadly gases. Iraq could decide any day to provide a biological or chemical weapon to a terrorist group."

Now Donald Rumsfeld began running his hand across his throat like Jack the Ripper. I gave him a what's with you look and moved on.

"The evidence also indicates Iraq is reconstituting its nuclear weapons program. Saddam has held numerous meetings with his scientists he calls the nuclear mujahedeen. Iraq has also attempted to purchase high-strength aluminum tubes and other equipment needed for gas centrifuges used to enrich uranium for nuclear weapons. That is why during any new United Nations inspections the Iraqis must reveal and destroy all existing weapons of mass destruction. And the inspectors must have access to any site, at any time, without pre-clearance, without delay, without exceptions. Saddam must disarm himself – or, for the sake of peace, we will lead a coalition to disarm him."

Comrade Condoleezza Rice clinched her hands and was grimacing while she prayed. Relax, Condi, I winked.

"We did not ask for this present challenge, but we accept it. We will meet the responsibility of defending human liberty. By our resolve, we will give strength to others. By our courage, we will give hope to others. And by our actions, we will secure the peace, and for the world a better day.

"'May God bless America.'

After that speech, which was so great I strutted off stage, my guys rushed around me and explained why they'd been acting weird: some evil person had loaded the teleprompter with the text of a speech I delivered October seventh, 2002. I'd have figured that out, anyway. You can't get over on W for long.

President Bush on Intelligent Design and War

I want you to understand what I'm about: I love God because He saved me from self-destruction as a drinker and selected me to lead this great nation. He has also told many others I should be president. These people are all believers and realize I have a special relationship with Him and every day give back by spreading His word and doing what He wants. I know He's happy every time I proclaim God created the Earth. That's commitment. That's righteousness.   And it's why recently I again stated my conviction that in education people should be exposed to different ideas. That's what learning is all about and why we must teach Intelligent Design in biology classes from sea to shining sea. We probably need another Scopes Trial. Evolution is only a theory. Why not present other theories? I know the liberals and the godless – who are usually the same – are going to shout that my science advisor, John H. Marburger III, said he doesn't "regard Intelligent Design as a scientific topic" and that "evolution is a cornerstone of modern biology." That's his opinion, that's his theory. So what?

I know millions of Americans agree with me. Many of them are on school boards in twenty-eight states where there are initiatives to offer an alternative to evolution. Evolution is bad for business. If we accept evolution we have to acknowledge either that there is no God or that He is subordinate to nature, and in either case we would have to concede that my policies are driven by something other than divine supernatural forces. This we must not permit.

Mine is a great mission, an unprecedented mission. My task is to civilize the world and transform every community on this God-built planet into something like Midland, Texas. For the everlasting benefit of non-Christian heathens, I'm going to democratize them. I believe in democracy. I believe in democracy for them. I don't much believe in democracy for myself, however, because when the other guy got more votes in 2000 that really wasn't God's will. He wanted the Electoral College to make the divine natural selection. He wanted George W. Bush to become president. His messengers on the Supreme Court and in Florida's most sacred political circles made it happen.

We must thank God I'm the one who's been in control. The other guy would have been a disaster. I knew what to do: I reduced very effective military operations where terrorists really existed, in Afghanistan, and lied about their existing in Iraq and started a war and created far more terrorists than I'd claimed were lurking there.

Every time a bomb blows up or maims American soldiers or Iraqi civilians or soldiers, my policies look even better. There's definitely an enemy out there. And don't tell me there's no Intelligent Design. The enemy is making bigger and better bombs all the time. He just killed fourteen marines with a blast that flipped their twenty-five-ton assault vehicle. The enemy has also taken to planting multiple explosives around the main bomb, and killing our guys when they go in to pick up the limbs and get design information about the blast.

I'm still ready to fight on. Well, not me, of course. I'm ready for the religious poor and working class people to keep fighting. I'm not like my dad, who fought in World War II. I'm like all my other relatives. I drum my chest on the sidelines. If I were actually in the war, I wouldn't have time to ravage this nation's wealth. It takes a lot of energy to make financial love to the Enron boys, "The Smartest Guys in the Room," and other larcenous, God-fearing Americans. Look around. God most loves liars and hypocrites and warmongers. He cherishes me and mine.

Saddam Hussein Meets Eminent Leader

My captors said I didn't have to. I assuredly knew that. They couldn't have forced me. They'd degraded me so many ways, true, but this was my choice. This I did because I, Saddam Hussein, eternal President of Iraq, wanted to continue to serve the people of my country. I thus agreed to be escorted from my cell and, in utmost secrecy, flown into the night.

I knew where I was going. Logically, where else could it be? I stepped off the plane into a hellish landscape and was driven past toy tombstones painted white by demonstrators, by the encampment of the bereaved-mother-turned-activist Cindy Sheehan, and into the compound of my most powerful enemy. Several stern men in suits escorted me to a tack room, told me to sit, and in a few minutes said stand as George W. Bush entered the room and examined me.

My English has been improving in prison but I knew we'd need an interpreter. This task was to be filled by a man who after fleeing Iraq years ago swindled millions of dollars in Jordan then skedaddled into Western embrace before being convicted of the crime, and in recent years generated much respect and excitement by lying to eager listeners about Iraqi weapons and intentions. For this service the United States government paid him several million a year. Now he's one of those clawing for power back home. In walked Ahmad Chalabi, and I shouted: "Pig."

Chalabi dutifully made the translation.

"Listen, Saddam," said Bush, "I know you're wondering why I've ordered you here."

"Not at all," I said.

"You mean you already know or you don't care."

"I assume you've brought me here to whip my ass at bike riding and golf."

"I could damn well do that, and in jogging and horse shoes, too. And we'll get to those things. First, though, I want to talk to you man to man about Iraq."

"I offered to debate that very subject before you invaded. You undoubtedly saw my interview with Dan Rather."

"I don't debate anything with anyone. I have political capital. But I'm willing to shoot the bull. I want what's best for Iraq and for America. Unless Iraq is secure then America is in danger."

"America is secure here and imperiled in Iraq."

"The only reason we're safe here is because I removed you from office."

"Don't imply I had any incriminating links to bin Laden or Al Qaeda or 9/11."

"You've murdered thousands in Iraq and Iran and Kuwait, and sometimes you used weapons of mass destruction to do so."

"Counsel has forbidden me to discuss my case."

"Fine. I just want to talk about the Iraq of today and tomorrow. We've got to get a democratic constitution in place. That can be the foundation of freedom in your country, and throughout the region, then the whole world. The Sunnis, your long-time supporters, are the only people who can prevent democracy from taking root."

"What you call democracy, I call aggression."

"Look at the democratic world and at your world. Forget politics. Just look."

"In my world they want strong leaders, not democrats."

"You're wrong. They want freedom."

"Who's they?"

"Just about everyone but the Sunnis, and even most of them."

"Even if, for argument, I accept your assertion, you still must account for the fearfully flawed draft of the constitution. Keep in mind, this constitution was written by Shiites and Kurds. Don't blame the Sunnis."

"They're the ones blowing people up."

"They're freedom fighters."

"They're terrorists."

"They believe in a secular state, much as the one I ruled."

"Secular murder," said Bush. "We're going to stay until there's secular freedom in Iraq."

"Don't delude yourself about a secular Iraq taking shape. It's quite the opposite, as every literate person knows. The Iraq you've created is chaotic and headed toward theocratic rule. Women in Basra have fewer rights today than when I was in command."

"You killed their husbands and sons and brothers whenever you wanted."

"I've killed no more of them than you did," I said.

"I don't look at it that way."

"Just remember, your grand constitution is laced with religion, and the theocrats will rule in a most reactionary way."

"I think you can help."

"Why should I help you?"

"Because we'll pay for your expertise."

"I'd need at least twice what Chalabi received."

"You got it."

"What would I have to do?"

"Just meet with Sunnis and other insurgents and convince them they can be free if they cooperate in the democratic process. Then let me know what they say."

"How can I do that from prison?"

"You can leave eight hours a day on a work-release program."

"Do I have to come to Crawford again?"

"No, don't worry. You can report to Chalabi. He'll be in the cell next to yours."

CHAPTER 3

Dick Cheney on Maintaining the Good Life

I am very well fed. Look at pictures of me a generation ago and you will see how I have been eating. I eat all the time. I have earned that right. I am the ultimate political operative in a land of wealth I both understand and control. True, I am not electable to the highest office but that does not matter. I am where I need to be. I am sitting by George W. Bush. He needs me now. He always has. He understands I know so much more.

I am expert on all significant matters both domestic and foreign. I was the youngest presidential chief of staff in history, for Gerald Ford, and I managed Ford's 1976 campaign, and served five terms as a Wyoming congressman and one year as House Minority Whip, and voted against a resolution demanding that Nelson Mandela be released from prison in South Africa because his African National Congress was a terrorist group that 'had a number of interests fundamentally inimical to the United States.' I was also a powerhouse advocate for the petroleum and coal industries of my state and the nation, and my unique experiences propelled me into the Pentagon, as Secretary of Defense, where I skillfully administrated the invasions of Panama and Kuwait and Iraq.

During much of the 1990's it was of course painful to see this nation in the arms of the libidinous President Clinton who was both "incoherent (and) inconstant (as he) squandered opportunities" and left us weak and vulnerable. Even though I was most busy as Chief Executive Officer of Halliburton for five years, I manufactured time in 1997 to found the Project for the New American Century. My comrades in arms were other brilliant parlor patriots like Donald Rumsfeld, Paul Wolfowitz, Eliot Abrams, and John Bolton.

We perceived that America had inalienable rights and duties as the preeminent power in the history of the world, and we articulated many quintessential tasks. The United States was manfully obligated to show "resolve to shape a new century favorable to American principles and interests." To do so, the nation would have to rebuild its defenses in order to dominate others through use of force, to establish democracies by military means, to launch preemptive wars, to fight multiple wars, to establish U.S. military bases in critical areas such the Persian Gulf states. And we were explicitly determined to take control of Iraq whether or not Saddam Hussein remained in power. Naturally, it would be beneficial if he stayed as a target. We further understood that our forces would with missionary zeal also have to perform extensive 'constabulary duties.' And we needed supremacy not merely on the ground. We needed unparalleled outer-space forces and missile defenses and Internet forces, and of course to have all that we needed to increase our already stratospheric defense spending by about twenty-five percent.

We knew what America needed. It needed what it desired. It desired enhancement of the most special lifestyle any people ever had. Our success was assured when George W. Bush selected me as his vice presidential running mate and we won in a judicial landslide. Early in our first term, the president asked me to direct the National Energy Policy Development Group. With a variety of energy experts including Ken Lay and other Enron executives and executives from other energy firms and numerous energy lobbyists, we forged policies that would enhance our pursuit of goals in the New American Century. These goals required lots of energy as well as money. These goals should have been confidential but two traitorous organizations, the Sierra Club and Judicial Watch, kept suing me for access to information about meetings, and I have battled them to suppress as much as possible. That is good policy.

People do not need to know this administration's ravenous pursuit of energy is depleting aquifers and creating big-truck traffic jams and smog in numerous recently pristine areas, including parts of my beloved Wyoming. They have no right to complain that our oil and gas acquisition teams have erected drilling rigs far more densely than tree huggers and other liberals would like. What do they really want except to complain? They certainly do not want to walk. And no solar or wind car is going to get their lazy asses wherever people like that go.

I go hunting and I know about guns. I also know about war. I have read a lot about it and talked a lot about it and often explained why it is so vital. That is why Joseph Wilson, our former ambassador to Iraq, should have been muzzled. He traveled and investigated and reported in 2003 that the president and I and others were wrong and deceitful in stating that Iraq was obtaining uranium for nuclear weapons from Niger. He was a traitor. You know what happens to traitors. High government officials leak that their wives are CIA agents. People are trying to tie this leak to my office. What a crock. Have you seen Wilson's wife Valerie Plame? She is no spook in hiding. She is a flashy blond posing for glossy shots with Wilson in their convertible and sitting at a restaurant table. They are trying to bring me down. They will not succeed. More than any man I understand America's greatest needs and how to fulfill them.

O'Reilly Clarifies Al Qaeda Remarks

Again, liberals are accusing me of being cruel and bigoted and having a dark heart. But those charges are insipid. Conservatives understand that. Bloodthirstiness is utterly unrelated to my declaration the armed forces shouldn't defend San Francisco if Al Qaeda attacks since citizens of that sinful city voted to restrict military recruiting on campuses. I wasn't really making a fatuous ideological statement. In fact I was crouching, opening wide, and firing my name onto the airwaves and through cyberspace and into your heads. I wanted some of you to agree with me. But not everyone. What I most need is a storm. Storms are news.

Hurricane O'Reilly is back again. That is essential. I am the top-rated ranter on cable TV. I didn't get that spot being rational and reasonable. I got it poking a finger in your liberal eye or stroking your right wing hot spots. I love being on top. Everyone knows who I am. Everyone says did you hear what O'Reilly just said. Attention is addictive. It's orgasmic. It's also a magnet for big bucks. It will be as long as I'm outrageous.

TV and radio are not my only sources of wealth, of course. If you're conservative, you know that. You're probably even a Premium Member of my website, a status offering an astonishing array of attractions. Click and see. Pay me $4.95 a month or $49.95 a year and you will receive at least fourteen listed benefits. They include listening to my Radio Factor show live and digging into ninety days of Archives, Podcasting, posting on the Message Boards, receiving exclusive Webcasts, scanning the O'Quiz Archive, checking out the Bill Photo Album, examining the O'Reilly Poll Archive, emailing Bill directly, trying to solve the brain-busters in the Crossword Archive, and much more.

And then there's The O'Reilly Store, a unique place to shop. You don't need to be a Premium Member to buy here but it would save you about ten percent. I know you'll want to load up on merchandise like Apparel, and Hats, and Bags & Totes, and Books, and Car & Truck accessories, and Home & Office supplies, and, naturally, Mugs. All political savants must buy Mugs. For $13.95 you can get a Mug emblazoned with No Spin Mom or Dad or Grandma or you can get one with my name on it.

Look sporty for the holidays and slip into my No Spin Varsity Jacket, a $149.95 value that Premium Members take home for a mere $134.95. My No Spin Fleece Vest is a steal at $35.95, and the O'Reilly Factor Sweatshirt is a most reasonable $39.95. A charming rascal like me naturally knows how to take care of the ladies, and I offer the No Spin Women's Hooded Sweatshirt at $39.95. Don't forget – you save on most of these garments with Premium Membership. But everyone pays only $16.95 for a line of stylish hats, all emblazoned with clever announcements. One of my favorites is The Spin Stops Here! Structured Baseball Cap.

You can also take me with you in your car. My Classic O'Reilly Factor Keychain is a pittance at $4.95, and imagine the pride you'll feel as fellow motorists read your $17.95 Spin Stops Here! License Plate Frame. Further enhance your automotive exterior with a Don't Be A Pinhead Bumper Sticker for $2.50.

When you get back to your fortified home, I'm sure you'll be carrying the $14.95 O'Reilly Factor Tote Bag laden with my literary classics "The O'Reilly Factor," "The No Spin Zone," "Who's Looking Out for You," "Those Who Trespass," and "The O'Reilly Factor for Kids." These epics can be yours for as little as $13.95 for a paperback. But don't be a tightwad. Get the autographed and personalized hardbacks for $39.95. We also offer a Who's Looking Out For You button three inches wide with my mug on it. "Pin it on your shirt or jacket with pride."

Cozy up next to your fireplace, crack open one of my books, and cover your cold feet with the $34.95 Spin Stops Here Fleece Blanket. Then underline your favorite passages with the pen from my $29.95 Spin Stops Here Metal Pen Box. If your roof springs a leak, don't worry and don't move. Simply open your $24.95 The Red Rain Stops Here Umbrella.

See, I can take better care of you than big government and for a lot less than your taxes.

President Bush Identifies Monolithic Terrorism

I have never been more confident during my worldwide battle against terrorism. I will never back down. I will never give in. I will settle for nothing less than complete victory. It's true that many soldiers and civilians have fallen and many more will. Tough days are certainly ahead. But ultimately only one thing matters: my determination is unshakable. I will take the fight to the terrorists. They know it and so do you and everyone else.

I am positive I'm right. I've got the support of most people. I don't care what pollsters say. They weren't at the Naval Academy last week when I delivered my "Strategy for Victory in Iraq" speech. The future officers clapped and roared like hell; I love being with warriors and they enjoy having me around. We understand each other. They know why I'm doing this. I also want you to understand. So I'm going to explain a few key passages from this critical speech.

My first urgent statement was that "the terrorists have made it clear that Iraq is the central front in their war against humanity, and so we must recognize Iraq as the central front in the war on terror." Don't listen to those who claim that I, George W. Bush, was in fact the one who insisted Iraq become the central front in the war on terror. How the hell did I do that? My liberal adversaries in the United States, and my fascist enemies in the Middle East, claim there was no terrorist activity in Iraq before I invaded in April 2003. Well, I say there was a terrorist threat, or at least terrorist thinking. And I could not tolerate their thinking terrorist thoughts. That would have been capitulation. Anyway, there damn sure are plenty of terrorists there now. And that proves my point.

My next huge statement was about Monolithic Terrorism. I declared, "Their objective is to drive the United States and coalition forces out of Iraq, and use the vacuum that would be created by an American retreat to gain control of that country. They would then use Iraq as a base from which to launch attacks against America, and overthrow moderate governments in the Middle East, and try to establish a totalitarian Islamic empire that reaches from Indonesia to Spain." That's exactly like the Domino Theory of Monolithic Communism. You remember that and know how it works. If Saigon falls, so does Wichita.

Nowadays that's why we're fighting these terrorists in Iraq. Otherwise, "they would be plotting and killing Americans across the world and within our own borders." Look at "those who blew up commuters in London and Madrid, murdered tourists in Bali, workers in Riyadh, and guests at a wedding in Amman." Let's get it straight. When bombs of the United States kill tens of thousands of civilians – or hundreds of thousands, as in Viet Nam – it's not merely okay, it's a righteous expression of democratic survival. But when those we bomb bomb us, it's diabolical. Ours is an "enemy without conscience – and they cannot be appeased." You've got to understand that. And I also want to note that the Spaniards were spineless for withdrawing from Iraq after being bombed. They're just asking to be bombed some more. That hasn't happened yet, but according to the Bush Doctrine, it surely will.

My next vital statement was that "free societies are peaceful societies," and in proof of that I offer my tranquil administration of this society. We are peaceful. We are very peaceful until we're attacked. When the Vietnamese attacked us, you saw what they got. When the Iraqis attacked us – when they fantasized about attacking us, I mean – thousands of them had to be slaughtered. We destroyed their bodies to save the souls of their surviving countrymen. It's a pretty big sacrifice, true, but necessary beyond dispute.

We have a comprehensive plan to enable the Iraqis to do for themselves what coalition forces are now doing. In fact, "coalition and Iraqi forces are on the offensive against the enemy, cleaning out areas controlled by the terrorists and Saddam loyalists, leaving Iraqi forces to hold territory taken from the enemy." Very soon, the Iraqi armed forces will be an independent fighting force. Already, the Iraqis have 120 army and police battalions of between 350 and 800 men, and 80 of those battalions are "fighting side-by-side with coalition forces, and about 40 others are taking the lead in the fight." Granted, there is only one independent Iraqi battalion now. But there will be more. They just need more time and training.

Evidently, those insurgents have so far had much more time and training. For that reason "we've increased our force levels in Iraq to 160,000 – up from 137,000 – in preparation for the December elections…America will help the Iraqis so they can protect their families and secure their free nation. We will stay as long as necessary to complete the mission. If our military tells me we need more troops, I will send them."

But remember, I've already emphasized Iraqi forces are improving. They must be strong or there will be civil war. There would certainly be civil war if we left now. Some say there is already civil war. Whatever you call the situation now, believe me, it would be far worse without my interference. I know that "setting an artificial deadline to withdraw would send a message across the world that America is a weak and an unreliable ally. Setting an artificial deadline to withdraw would send a signal to our enemies – that if they wait long enough, America will cut and run and abandon its friends. And setting an artificial deadline to withdraw would vindicate the terrorists' tactics of beheadings and suicide bombings and mass murder – and invite new attacks on America. To all who wear the uniform, I make you this pledge: America will not run in the face of car bombers and assassins so long as I am you Commander-in-Chief.'"

The Midshipmen erupted. They understand what's going on, unlike the weaklings in America and Iraq who claim that some Iraqi security forces are currently mass murdering people in the style of a Saddam. I don't like to talk about that. It's probably a lie or exaggeration. And you know damn well I don't like to talk about withdrawal. Others have been doing that. The day I spoke, the National Security Council published a policy paper that predicted "a reduction in the U.S. military presence in 2006." A couple of days before that the Pentagon said we'd bring home about 20,000 troops after the elections this month. And according to news reports, "the White House said on November 26 that Democratic Senator Joseph Biden's plan for a 50,000 troop drawdown next year was remarkably similar to its own."

I didn't say that. I don't talk like that. I will never back down. I will never give in. I will take the fight to the terrorists. I will settle for nothing less than complete victory.

Rove Seeks to Preserve King George

It is time for an enlightened change in the Constitution of the United States of America. We must forever demolish the twenty-second amendment which states no man can be elected president more than two times. That limitation, in the case of our current leader, George W. Bush, is intolerable. We must act to make him permanently eligible to be our commander in chief.

The twenty-second amendment was created to prevent some future president – like Franklin D. Roosevelt – from institutionalizing the dangerous belief that government can, and indeed should, help the people in ways private industry cannot. That childish, even communistic, notion has many times been discredited, most recently after Hurricane Katrina when an inept government and passive citizenry, still paralyzed by the socialist spirit of Roosevelt, were unable to perform rescue operations as well as unsupervised corporations could have.

The twenty-second amendment was certainly not intended to deprive us of the ongoing service of a truly great leader. Therefore, ladies and gentlemen, we now have the obligation to, in effect, sign an eternal contract with the man God wants to be President of the United States. This is in every way a divine opportunity. George W. Bush will only be sixty years old in 2006. He is a fit and sober specimen who can be expected to live at least thirty more years, each of which must be used in holy executive service of the United States of America.

Only by preserving the presidency of George W. Bush will we be certain to wage relentless war against terrorists and other hellish creatures. At this moment, in fact, the president is diligently preparing us to believe that Syria and Iran are planning to attack the United States, or at least develop the capability to do so, and we must attack them first.

In spiritual terms, sustaining President Bush would guarantee maintaining a righteous populace that fears sex but is unafraid of tall tales of environmental damnation. We'd also ensure a manly executive style of talking loudly and studying little. We need confidence and bold action, not timidity and bookishness.

Our international prestige today underscores the efficacy of the leadership of George W. Bush. We must not relinquish what we have. Even when the tragic moment inevitably does come, and President Bush is no longer able to physically lead us in our many battles, we need only enshrine him in a modern pyramid and forever listen to his recorded sermons that show the way.

Osama bin Laden Speaks to America

I have just amended my speech, and will at times speak to you spontaneously and from the heart. I must do so now for I do not have long. Examine my face, once described by women of the Middle East as handsome or cool, and you will see that I am not a healthy man. I'm gaunt and gray and may have kidney problems and certainly have endured a selfless and eternal battle against you infidels. I know you are hunting me. Perhaps you will find me before my body independently expires. I do not care.

I am isolated in caves and tents and under the stars and in the most filthy and modest of homes, and for too long have been unable to speak to you on video tape. Meanwhile, dedicated but lesser men such as Ayman al-Zawahari, the former physician who became my assistant in Afghanistan, and Zarqawi, my Al Qaeda leader in Iraq, are now much more active. And why have I not been more involved, you may ask? It's essential I martyr others rather than myself.

Nevertheless, I am at last willing to step into sunlight and offer you a long-term truce. You stop occupying our countries and killing us and we will stop killing you in our homelands and attacking you in America. How could I possibly enforce such a diplomatic decree? Don't tell me that would be like an arsenic-laced Napoleon issuing orders from his island prison. I refuse to think that way. Naturally, I consider myself leader of the international coalition against America. That is why I presume to guarantee that if you don't respond, "Your minds will be troubled and your lives embittered… We have nothing to lose. A swimmer in the ocean does not fear the rain. You have occupied our lands, offended our honor and dignity and let our blood and stolen our money and destroyed our houses…and we will give you the same treatment.

"You have tried to prevent us from leading a dignified life, but you will not be able to prevent us from a dignified death. Failing to carry our jihad, which is called for in our religion, is a sin. The best death to us is under the shadows of swords. Don't let your strength and modern arms fool you. They win a few battles but lose the war.

Patience and steadfastness are much better. We were patient in fighting the Soviet Union with simple weapons for ten years and we bled their economy and now they are nothing.

"In that there is a lesson for you."

You see why enemy forces hunt me without cease. I can kill with planes or words, and am by bounds the most articulate man in this war. All Bush and Cheney have said is they don't negotiate with terrorists. They only destroy them. So how will this war ever end? You won't negotiate with those you are fighting, and your leaders forever insist – their need for enemies is as unrelenting as mine – that you are indeed in a real war. Of course, if a nation as vast as America really were at war, wouldn't it have ten percent of its population under arms, as during World War Two? Instead, you struggle, and often fail, to meet even the most modest recruiting requirements. And yet you're talking evermore of also attacking Iran. I hope you will not do that but have always considered your invasion of Iraq a preliminary step to assaulting our Muslim brothers to the east.

At this instant I for the first time foresee that even in abject hiding I can do much more than infrequently deliver tapes of appalling technical quality. I really do understand America. And I know you would never negotiate with me. So if you agree to negotiate with leaders who were not involved in September Eleventh, pursuant to withdrawing from Muslim territories in exchange for our vow not to attack you at home or anywhere else, I will send you my dissipated head on a golden platter.

2006

CHAPTER 4

Fortress America and The Long War

We must all be thankful I am President of the United States. If a Democrat or lesser Republican were in office, we wouldn't be so secure despite now facing threats more dangerous to this country than Nazi Germany and Imperial Japan combined. Be assured. I am preparing us very well for The Long War. We're going to have to fight battles worldwide for at least twenty years in order to defeat the terrorists. For that we need to be alert and powerful. And I'm going to lay it all out here for you, so you can sleep at night.

On the international front, we will continue to attack as many nations as possible. And we'll also target unfriendly media outlets like al-Jazeera. I shouldn't have let weaklings talk me out of that one. Don't you realize the terrorists would blow up Fox News if they could? Why shouldn't we do the same stuff? We'll bomb their TV studios and dining rooms and bedrooms and anywhere else they could be, and if they aren't really there, that's too bad. We're lashing out, period. Right now that means we're going to continue to kill thousands of enemies, and women and children, in Iraq and Afghanistan. And we're going to torture prisoners there and anywhere else we want, and anyone who says we shouldn't doesn't understand war like I do.

And most importantly, we're working hard getting ready to hit Iran. We're going to have to, you know. Their president wants to destroy Israel and he'll soon have the means to do so. If I don't step between them, the Israelis will launch a massive preemptive nuclear strike, and I wouldn't be able to stop them. It's better that I do the hitting, in a controlled and humane way. I see an intense conventional bombing campaign lasting one month, as originally planned, but a lot longer once things get going. We'll bombard their nuclear facilities, and let's face it, we'll be taking out lots of other things too. We have very smart bombs but collateral damage is inevitable, something for the Iranian government to keep in mind. Once we've bombed enough to possibly destroy the nuclear facilities, we'll send in troops to examine, and if necessary demolish, what's left of those places. But we won't try to occupy a vast nation twice as big as Texas and inhabited by seventy million Muslims. I'll still dig my boots in in Iraq, and probably Syria later on, but not in Iran. That shows perspective and restraint my political opponents say I lack.

After awhile we'll be free to strike North Korea. I am worried about what'll happen to Seoul but not nearly as much as I am about any city here. If you were President of the United States, you'd have to look at it the same way. As you know, I have a visceral reaction every time I think about that little bastard Kim Jong-il. Of course I'm hoping the Chinese will tell him no more food or energy if he continues nuclear weapons development. He's probably already got a few nukes. Why don't the Chinese do something? Don't worry. I'm not going to attack them or my undemocratic buddy Vladimir Putin in Soviet Russia. Vladimir's a good guy and not nearly as bad as Stalin, anyway.

As leader of this international battle for survival, it is my right and my duty to listen to your telephone conversations, and not only if you're an Arab or of Arab ancestry. If you've talked to an Arab, we'll also listen. If you're a member of a radical left wing organization – that is one whose members disagree with me about any issue – watch what you say. We'll tap your home phones, your office phones, your cell phones. We'll read your snail mail and your email. We're going to open up your Google files and examine every subject searched. If you've read about the Iranian soccer team, you might hear a cold-night knock on your door if we don't kick it in first. We'll prod you, question you, and if necessary we'll pull your underwear and see what's inside. What have you been buying? Which movies are you renting? Who've you been doing business with? Those are rhetorical questions. We already know. Your credit card activity is vital to maintaining national security, and therefore my special place in history.

What else is essential to complete our Fortress America? How do we insulate ourselves from this largely nonwhite world of savages? We've got a helluva start right on our southern border. We're building a wall. In the American way, and especially in our Texas style, we're erecting the greatest wall in history. It'll be longer and wider than the Great Wall of China, more righteous than the Berlin Wall, and harder to scale than the sides of Masada. It'll seal us off from Latino aliens and Muslim terrorists burrowing in their midst. And the wall will go up faster than hell. We're assembling a huge unarmed army of illegal workers to do the job, which doesn't pay enough for our citizens. We could do the same thing up north in Canada, but that would be an awful long wall. Maybe we'll annex Canada and let the North Pole be our defensive perimeter up there. I can't imagine Osama and his boys coming in that way.

What about our ocean coastlines? I don't think we'll build walls along them. Instead, we'll either search or sink every ship that approaches our shores. Clearly, it isn't tough enough to merely be unassailable along our perimeter. We must also put a roof over Fortress America. Our air force is already capable of dominating the low skies. And once we have thousands of anti-ballistic missiles in every state and our nuclear space weapons are deployed, we'll be everywhere invulnerable and forever free.

President Bush Celebrates Three Years in Iraq

Hello, Cleveland. I'm thrilled to be here. I've always loved Cleveland and never so much as today as we celebrate the third anniversary of Operation Iraqi Freedom, my war to liberate our friends, and indeed the entire world, from terrorism. I'm the only man strong and righteous enough to save civilization. That's why I told my speechwriters to write terrorism five, ten, or fifteen times per page. Write terrorism until you're either terrified or too tired to refute me. Don't stop with terror. Write Al Qaeda several times per page. That always helps, especially when justifying my Iraq attack. And now that things are going so well over there, it's great to fill my speeches with resounding references to the Iraqi army and Iraqi forces and the Iraqi police. They'll get you thinking the right way.

You've got to have perspective, so I'm going to tell you about Tal Afar. Tal Afar is a microcosm of Iraq. Tal Afar had been a terrorist stronghold where kidnappings and beheadings were common until we attacked and ran the terrorists off. But when we left, Iraqi forces at the time weren't strong enough to maintain security and Tal Afar again became a dying city as terrorists, and their hateful ideology, violated mosques and schools and everyone in Tal Afar. In response, Iraqi and coalition forces carefully prepared Operation Restoring Rights. They wiped out surrounding places terrorists might hide and built a big dirt wall around Tal Afar. Iraqi forces then attacked and in two weeks, aided a little by us, killed and arrested hundreds of terrorists. Tal Afar is now a great place and will soon be comparable to Cleveland. People need to know about Tal Afar and think about it often. To help you focus, I've referred to Tal Afar about forty times in my speech.

Why would you want to think about Baghdad? That's negative and limited. I'm hoping you won't dwell on thousands of casualties in the capital and elsewhere in the country if I can keep you thinking about happy Tal Afar and terrible terrorists and powerful Iraqi soldiers and police and security forces. I've got to keep you thinking the right way for a very long time. I've committed to that. Yes, you heard it. American forces will be in Iraq beyond the final day of my presidency and it will be up to future presidents to withdraw them.

Many of you have accused me of being a liar and an idiot. You're for sure wrong about the latter. First, you'll never hear me saying "civil war" forty times in a speech. And second, by keeping our working-class soldiers in Iraq until the end of my presidency, no one will ever be able to say I lost Iraq. I won Iraq. I deposed Saddam. I established democracy there and promoted it throughout the region. There's still a chance I'll go down in history as a great man, a visionary. And even if that doesn't happen, it's better we stay and thousands more die than President George W. Bush be labeled a loser.

Bush Watches *The Battle of Algiers*

Last night my entourage and I wanted to watch a Sylvester Stallone movie, something exciting with lots of action and explosions, but we didn't have one in the White House and couldn't wait for a rental so I said okay when a guest from the CIA claimed he had a good one for us, *The Battle of Algiers*. I almost didn't let him show it when he added, "It's an old black and white film with characters speaking French and Arabic."

"How the heck will we understand?"

"Subtitles."

"I hate reading anything, especially those confusing subtitles."

"Don't worry. You'll feel this story."

"Fine, start it up," I said.

They begin in 1957 with some skinny old Algerian man who can barely stand because he's been tortured a long time by the French. I'd forgotten the French could be tough but of course I don't approve since I never allow torture. It sure can work, though. This guy tells the police where the top terrorist is hiding; he and his family are inside a wall, like a cave, in an old building in the ancient Casbah section of Algiers. The police tell him he's surrounded and has to come out.

The movie then jumps back three years, and it turns out this guy, Ali La Pointe, has been a criminal since childhood.

"Hold it right there," I said. "That figures. Terrorists are cowards who prey on law-abiding citizens."

"Mr. President," said the CIA agent, "the French had been occupying Algeria for almost a hundred thirty years. By 1954 there were a million French colonials in the country. And keep in mind that between 1830 and 1890 the native population declined from four million to two-and-a-half million."

"How'd that happen?" I asked.

"The French came in and tried to force their religion, culture, economics, education and politics on people they considered inferior."

"The French were trying to give them democracy and a better life."

"That was hardly the case, Mr. President. The French wouldn't

64

even allow the Algerians to have public meetings. It's pretty hard for a democracy to take hold under those circumstances."

"Go ahead, roll it."

The movie then says in 1956 the French ban drugs and alcohol, and they use the guillotine on second offenders. (That's even tougher than three strikes.) All this time the Algerian terrorist group – the FLN – is shooting police in the street. Naturally, the French seal off the Arab Quarter and search everyone and demand a ready ID. They have to. Terrorists are pulling pistols from women's robes and fruit stands and boxes on trees, and shooting more French policemen.

I cheer during the next scene when French authorities respond by planting a bomb on a narrow stone street in the Casbah. That isn't terroristic; that's righteous. Sure, lots of women and children are killed. But let me tell you, my bombs are bigger than that. The bombs have to be big to teach simple people the basic truths. And they still won't listen. Three Arab women cut their hair and put on makeup to look like real Western ladies so they can get through checkpoints without hassle. And these terrorists take their bombs to a guy who activates them, and the women then plant the bombs in a café, a disco, and an airport.

"See all those French civilians getting killed?"

"Mr. President," replied the agent, "the French killed between four hundred thousand and a million citizens of Algeria, a place they had no right to be."

That's what it takes. Look, thank God. French paratroopers are arriving. They're really smart and well-trained, just like our guys, and they're figuring out the terrorists usually don't know more than three others, the one who brings them into the FLN and the two they bring in. It's a bunch of independent triangles. But the French know what to do. They interrogate with a capital I. And they break a general strike with early-morning raids into the Casbah, rounding up "dirty Arabs" and forcing them to get back to work. The radio reminds Algerians that "France is your Motherland (and to) resist the FLN."

The French are really taking it to the FLN, beating prisoners, holding their heads under water, burning them with blow torches, hanging them upside down, and attaching electric cables to their ears. The terrorists still don't get it. They drive through pretty French areas of Algiers and machinegun well-dressed folks. That stuff doesn't work against a democracy. The French intensify torture and brutality, and Ali La Pointe is now the only terrorist left. In the end, as at the start, he is surrounded inside his cave wall. He has thirty seconds to come out. He doesn't, so the French attach explosives and blow the place up, and, by God, that ends the bombing network, and Algiers becomes fairly quiet.

That only lasts a couple of years, though, and the desperate French bring back World War II tough guy General Charles De Gaulle to lead the nation. But he soon betrays his country by concluding the war can't be won and offering the Algerians a referendum on their future. Almost a hundred percent of them want the French out. I'll bet no more than eighty percent of Iraqis want us out.

Hillary Communes with George

"I'm proud to tell you, as I have so many others, that I've always been a praying person," said Hillary Rodham Clinton.

"I might believe that now," replied George W. Bush, "but there's no way you were in college."

"I certainly was."

"I hear you used to walk around campus, carrying books by Marx and Lenin and Mao."

"Those were strictly for class. Besides, I always had a bible in my purse. At Yale you definitely weren't a praying person."

"I was praying my damn hangovers would go away. Listen, I've admitted I didn't turn my life over to Jesus until I was forty. And thank God, He's saved me and continues to guide me in a profound spiritual way. Democrats are jealous of my divine access."

"I'm not like most of them," she said. "I talk about religion more every year, and pretty soon God's name will be in my speeches as much as in yours. Many times I actually feel like a preacher in the pulpit as I urge my parishioners to not merely accept religious people but to embrace them and rejoice that they have the conviction to 'live out their faith in the public square.'"

"Amen. That's exactly why Republicans have been beating Democrats. We stand for things, like no abortion."

"I'm also strong on that issue. Don't pretend otherwise. I've gone before pro-choice groups and told them that abortion is 'a sad, even tragic choice for many women (and that) religious and moral values' enable many teenage girls to say no to libidinous boys."

"Like your husband."

"Exactly."

"I think you Democrats are trying to move in on Middle America."

"We are Middle America."

"You were. Now most of you are clinging to godless regions along the coasts."

"Not anymore. We're conquering the new moral high ground, just as the 'religious left' has so often done. We were the leaders of anti-slavery crusades and the New Deal and the civil rights movement. Now I'm leading the fight against immigrants invading this country. 'I am, you know, adamantly against illegal immigrants…People have to stop hiring them.' I'm going to make sure we enhance border security. 'There's technology now available…advanced radar systems…and other identification systems that we've been very slow to deploy and unwilling to spend money on.'"

"You're not as strong as I am on immigration," he said. "I'm sending thousands of National Guard troops to strengthen our border."

"You're pretty damn late. You and your Republican big-business cronies are the ones hiring illegal immigrants. They wouldn't be here otherwise."

"How many nominees in your husband's administration were lost because they'd hired illegal nannies?"

"That wouldn't happen in a Hillary Clinton administration. And beware – I'm just as formidable on defense. I backed your Iraq war resolution in 2002 and have since steadfastly reiterated my support. We must give the Iraqis plenty of time to stabilize their government and train powerful security forces."

"No one's as determined to help Iraq as I am."

"You're amazing, all right. Not many who've done what you've done would have the brass to fly into the Green Zone last month and face the troops and declare we must not forget the danger of a post-September-11th world and that Iraq is a front in the war on terror and the terrorists who harm those who love freedom."

"America is safer and the world is better off because of my actions," he said.

"Because of my inaction, I obviously agree. I wasn't one of those Senate weaklings, like John Kerry and Russ Feingold, who tried to pass the pitiful plan to pull out all U.S. troops over the next thirteen months."

"Thanks for your patriotism. You're morally tough and no doubt physically tough as well and you're a great American. I have no doubt you'll whip that wimp John Kerry and any other Democrat in your primary."

"Kerry isn't man enough to accept that so far it's been necessary to kill more than fifty thousand Iraqi civilians," she said.

"We didn't kill all of them. The terrorists or the insurgents, whatever, killed even more than we did."

"We had to do it. Thank God we have a man of your charm and charisma leading this nation."

"You really should be a Republican, Hillary."

"In many ways, I already am."

Ahmadinejad Debates George W. Bush

President Ahmadinejad – President Bush, thank you for at last responding to my letter to you, which I wrote in May 2006. I thought perhaps you were overwhelmed by my logic and could offer no refutation.

President Bush – Don't kid yourself. I just didn't want to communicate with a terrorist.

PA – And I, sir, am more than equally aggrieved talking to a warmonger. Shall we proceed with the points in my letter?

PB – Go ahead.

PA – I started by asking how you, an avowed follower of Jesus Christ and one who supposedly respects human rights and claims he's battling terror worldwide, reconcile your religious beliefs with your actions, which include attacking countries on the flimsy pretext of their having weapons of mass destruction, killing scores of thousands of their people, destroying their water sources, agriculture and industry, and at the same time ruining the lives of thousands of your own soldiers, whose hands are "stained with the blood of others" and who daily commit suicide and suffer depression and battle a myriad of debilitating ailments.

PB – Don't lecture me that it's bad to end the brutal dictatorship of Saddam Hussein. In the 1980's your country lost hundreds of thousands of its bravest young men in a war Saddam started and that lasted eight bloody years.

PA – At the time, your nation was ardently backing its good friend Saddam.

PB – Things change, and they change rapidly, don't they, President Ahmadinejad? Let me tell the Iranian people – they'll receive this uncensored, won't they? – that after 9/11 my administration and many Americans appreciated the support Iran gave our country. Iran allowed our airplanes to use some of its bases after they returned from battling our then common enemy – Al Qaeda – in Afghanistan. You also used your contacts in northern and western Afghanistan to help us get some allies there. You wanted someone to take out the

Taliban and didn't want to do it yourselves. We did it for you. And you had a desperate desire for Saddam to be removed, but couldn't do it yourselves. That's why Iran helped us conclude – incorrectly, it turns out – that Iraq had WMDs and that the Iraqis would view us as liberators. My administration responded just like you wanted us to. As I recount this, I almost feel like your patsy.

PA – Let me remind you, I did not become president until August 2005. Those were not my policies.

PB – They probably would've been.

PA – That's speculative. Furthermore, many in your government are saying now, were in fact saying then, that Iran was an even more dangerous enemy than Iraq.

PB – You are. And about your nuclear program…

PA – Excuse me, President Bush, let us deal with that later in the discussion, as our staffs agreed last week.

PB – You're damn sure going to have to deal with it at some point.

PA – Mr. President, you have prisoners in Guantanamo Bay who have no lawyers, who cannot see their families, who are being held and tortured without even being charged. "There's no international monitoring of their conditions and fate. No one knows whether they are prisoners, POWs, accused or criminals…I fail to understand how such actions correspond to…the teachings of Jesus Christ (Peace Be Upon Him), human rights and liberal values."

PB – We're holding terrorists who aren't combatants in a real war.

PA – You and your administration daily insist you're at war. How, then, do you justify ignoring the laws of the Geneva Convention and stripping people of their most fundamental legal rights.

PB – (President Bush reaches into his shirt pocket and pulls out a newspaper article in English, accompanied by a specially-prepared Farsi translation.)

Here you are, President Ahmadinejad, great defender of human liberty. Do you recognize that pretty girl in the picture? Of course you do. Millions do. And after today, billions will know. Her name is Atefah Sahaaleh. Two years ago this month she was executed at age sixteen. What had she done? She'd had sexual relations with her boyfriend, and maybe another guy or two, and she'd been raped by a middle-aged and married revolutionary guard named Ali Darabi, whose brutal crime the court declared her fault. She'd broken your sacred Sharia law by "committing acts incompatible with chastity." Then, while arguing for her life against a bloodthirsty judge, she'd ripped off her hijab. For history, let's note that judge's name – Haji Rezai. He accelerated the pace of judicial murder – just three months from arrest to execution – because he said the town "Neka was becoming lax and immoral and he wanted to clean it up, particularly because it was the summer months, and lots of tourists were stopping off."

At six a.m. the town square of Neka was full of people who wanted a good show. Judge Haji Rezai made sure they got it. He personally put the noose around Atefah's neck and ordered the crane to lift her. The great Haji Rezai then insisted that the young lady – whose mother was already long dead, whose father was a heroin addict and of no use, and whose brother had drowned – be left hanging there in the wretched square for forty-five minutes.

How does your God justify that, President Ahmadinejad? How does your God explain Sharia law setting nine-years old as the female age of consent, and of criminal liability. How does your God account for that?

PA – I must again emphasize that you're talking about something that took place a year before I became president. This young woman had received some jail time and a hundred lashes for a similar transgression. A similar punishment should have sufficed this time.

I'd like to emphasize that in April of this year I "announced that a ruling which prevented women from watching men playing sports in stadiums would soon be reversed." And that week I also "objected to punishment of women appearing in stadiums without a proper hijab." What happened? Several of the nation's most powerful ayatollahs protested and demanded I cancel the order. Numerous clerics demonstrated. I had to retreat.

PB – Then you blamed it on an American conspiracy.

PA – You know politics.

PB – I know you and the reactionary political and religious elements in your country routinely muzzle the press, and harass and arrest and torture dissidents.

PA – They're better treated than those at Guantanamo Bay.

PB – I'm talking about your own citizens, and those who've committed no crimes.

PA – We have a sovereign right, indeed a sacred obligation, to protect the Islamic Revolution against those who tarnish it. After my election victory last year I swore that "a new Islamic Revolution has arisen and will, if God wills, cut off the roots of injustice in the world."

PB – What are you, some sort of Messiah in charge of a theocracy?

PA – You, President Bush, are the man daily criticized by many of your own people for having a messianic complex. And regarding theocracies, none is more fanatical than your administration.

PB – You're calling the United States a theocracy?

PA – Yes, and Israel, too. You claim God has chosen you to liberate the world and, in particular, to democratize the people of the Middle East. How, then, do you justify backing wholly undemocratic nations like Egypt, Jordan, and Saudi Arabia, and opposing those with at least the beginnings of democracy, like Palestine and Lebanon.

PB – The last two are hotbeds of terrorism. Look at the suicide bombings in, and coming from, Gaza and the West Bank.

PA – Look at the repression there by the Israeli theocrats.

PB – Israel's a beacon of democracy in the Middle East.

PA – Israel is a terroristic state that must change its behavior.

PB – President Ahmadinejad, how do you, as a man who feels himself chosen by God to "cut off the roots of injustice in the world," justify your hateful and asinine comments implying the Holocaust did not happen?

PA – I merely stated that evidence is lacking.

PB – We could stack hundreds of thousands of corpses on your desk. How's that? Have you seen the film clips? Have your read the endless testimony of survivors as well as Nazi perpetrators?

PA – At this stage I am perhaps willing to acknowledge, at least tacitly, that the Holocaust occurred. But what has that to do with the people of the Middle East? Permit me to read to you from my letter: "Throughout history, many countries have been occupied, but I think the establishment of a new country with a new people, is a new phenomenon that is exclusive to our times…Sixty years ago (Israel) did not exist… Old documents and globes" show no trace of "a country named Israel… Does that logically translate into the establishment of the state of Israel in the Middle East or support for such a state?

"I am sure you know how – and at what cost – Israel was established: many thousands were killed in the process; millions of indigenous people were made refugees; hundreds of thousands of hectares of farmland, olive plantations, towns and villages were destroyed. This tragedy is not exclusive to the time of establishment; unfortunately it has been ongoing for sixty years now."

PB – Regarding the statement you just made, as well as your public talk about "wiping Israel off the map" or "wiping Israel away," I'm going to tell you straight out, and I've said it before: the United States will use military force to ensure the survival of our friend, ally, and ideological brother Israel.

You're a hateful anti-Semite.

PA – I'm no such thing. Are you not aware that I appointed many Jews to high positions in my government? I'm not anti-Semitic. I'm anti-Zionist. I'm unhappy about the existence of Israel, true, but more so I'm appalled by the domination of Palestine by an artificial state. There can be no peace with an obscene wall slicing through the towns and souls of people on the West Bank. There will be no rest as long as Israel behaves like Hitler, who "sought pretexts to invade other nations… (just as) the Zionist regime is now seeking baseless pretexts to invade Islamic countries."

The Europeans should provide a homeland for the Jews. According to your historical information, that would be their moral obligation. America could also provide a homeland. The Middle East is an illogical place.

PB – The Middle East is the only place for Israel. The nation is already almost sixty years old. Many sacrifices have been made to build and sustain this heroic state. Your talk of removing Jews from the region is irresponsible and unrealistic. That also applies to Hezbollah and Hamas.

PA – Israel could not sustain itself long term without America.

PB – Israel's got America, and you better accept it.

PA – Then you better accept that the wall in the West Bank has got to come down and those settlements have to be abandoned. Either that, or no peace.

PB – Stop the terrorism, stop supporting and arming Hezbollah, for example, and I think Israel will give back most of the West Bank.

PA – Most isn't enough.

PB – Right, no matter what Israel gives back, the surrounding nations are going to want more. First return the West Bank, then give us the rest of Israel. It's not going to happen. And you're not getting nuclear weapons.

PA – We have many times stated we're not seeking nuclear weapons, only nuclear energy.

PB – Those statements are lies.

PA – You lie. We lie.

PB – God knows what the truth is.

PA – "Those with insight can already hear the sounds of the shattering and fall of the ideology and thoughts of the Liberal democratic systems. We increasingly see that people around the world are flocking towards a main focal point – that is the Almighty God. Undoubtedly through faith in God and the teachings of the prophets, the people will conquer their problems. My question for you is: 'Do you want to join them?'"

PB – I'm confident that God will in fact continue to protect Western democratic ideals and those who support them. And I can prove it.

PA – How?

PB – God will proclaim who is right.

PA – Fine, let's go talk to Him right now.

Straight Talk from Condoleezza Rice

Let me explain: counter-terrorism adviser Richard Clarke had many opportunities to tell us about his concerns during 2001, and he failed to do so. I stated that for the record and was later flabbergasted Clarke claimed he'd sent me an urgent memo on January 24, 2001, when I was National Security Adviser and responsible for terroristic matters. I don't remember reading the memo. Someone must have misplaced it.

Furthermore, I can assure you, as I did the 9/11 Commission, that CIA chief George Tenet did not have any "so-called emergency meeting" with me about the imminent and ominous intentions of Al Qaeda in July 2001. It's "incomprehensible" I would have forgotten such a critical encounter. I also need to emphasize there shouldn't have even been a 9/11 Commission. We're at war, and national security secrets must not be discussed outside the office of President George W. Bush. Consequently, I'm chagrined that my State Department recently conceded there had in fact been a meeting between a worried Tenet and me. He must have been quite vague and unconvincing. At any rate, this briefing wouldn't have been necessary if the irresponsible President Clinton and his cronies had been on the terrorist ball the previous eight years.

We, by contrast, were at our battle stations throughout June and July of 2001. Nevertheless, we could not have predicted Al Qaeda would try to use airplanes as missiles. Those who sent memos to President Bush, warning him of just such an attack, were not credible. The only credible account is our own. We greatly increased funding for counter-terrorism, and continue to ignore news that in 2001 the administration "vetoed a request to divert $800 million from missile defense into counterterrorism." That is preposterous.

The administration of President Bush is supernaturally strong against terrorism and determined to extirpate it. Still, as compassionate conservatives, we tried to reason with Saddam Hussein. Many times in 2002 and early 2003 I assured the nation and the world that we were seeking a peaceful solution and were in a diplomatic mode. Richard Haas, the president's policy planning director at the State Department, claimed he had a meeting with me in July 2002 and questioned making Iraq our focus since there were, he insisted, much more important concerns about terror; he said I told him the decision to attack had already been made.

Suppose it had: we could not forever offer the olive branch, could we? Saddam Hussein and his Iraqi henchmen were building some of the most destructive weapons in history. In September 2002 I stated that Iraqi aluminum tubes were "only really suited for nuclear weapons... (and) we don't want the smoking gun to be a mushroom cloud." Vice President Dick Cheney agreed, emphasizing the tubes were the most damning evidence that Iraq had resumed making nuclear weapons. The CIA was also behind us, and I said, "If Tenet, the CIA director, had any misgivings, he never shared them with the White House." I do not know why Stephen Hadley, my top aide at the time, claimed he received two memos from the CIA and a phone call from Tenet in October 2002 warning him that evidence Iraq was trying to obtain uranium in Africa was unreliable. They said they sent me a memo, and the president also got one. I must not have read the memo. Or perhaps I did not read all of it. Neither did the president. It did not matter. We were at war.

I understand war and have read a lot about it in both English and Russian. How many people do you know who've read *War and Peace* in the language of Tolstoy? I have great historical insight. I was raised in Birmingham, Alabama in the 1950's and 60's and have personally felt the whip of racial discrimination. That is why I so much admire the "hardness and determination" of the Israelis. In the 1930's, long before the Holocaust, they annexed Arab land and murdered opponents and, with British help, cut off social services and job opportunities for those who had lived there for generations and, in a paradigm of segregation, forced thousands of Arabs to leave. I usually do not explain things in quite that way. It's easier to be self-righteous than fair. Three years ago my convictions enabled me to warn Syria to end its occupation of Lebanon and to be prepared to verify it did not have weapons of mass destruction. I ignored those who pointed out the hypocrisy of this position since Israel has scores of atomic weapons.

I do not like thinking about the Arab perspective, so I don't talk much about the countless thousands of Iraqi women and children who've been killed or maimed by our Holy War. Do not think, however, that I'm unaffected by the bloody and endless nature of our democratic crusade in Iraq. In fact, I am most unhappy about it. Now I won't be able to run for president until at least 2012.

Bush's New Language about War

Absolutely we're winning the war and achieving our objectives. I'm not in denial. I know the facts. Our casualties are escalating and so are Iraqi civilian casualties. That's just part of our long, hard, and bloody road to peace. We can win only by continuing to stagger down that road.

I'm helping everyone understand. We aren't stay-the-course fools. We're flexible and dynamic. We axed old phrases and are trumpeting the new. We're constantly changing, believe me, even if we look like aging statues.

I admit, even though we're winning, I'm not satisfied with the war. The best indication of that is I've sort of accepted the principle of a timeline for our getting out of Iraq. I've hinted there might be an end to this for us even without the absolute victory I've obsessively guaranteed. We'll probably have to declare Iraqi security forces are ready, then start pulling out. I'm not going to officially admit this, of course. I'm going to keep hoping we'll have permanent military bases in Iraq. But that's up to the Iraqi government. We can't predict what they'll do. And frankly, their current government probably won't be around much longer.

I won't be around, either, as president. I'll be retired. So what I want most is to creatively and dynamically pretend I'm not pretending so I can keep the fight for peace going until I'm out in January 2009. Then when the catastrophe-in-waiting inevitably happens, I'll blame my weak Democratic successor, who undoubtedly lacks my credentials as warrior and statesman.

Supreme Power

Yesterday, Prime Minister Nuri Kamal al-Maliki made this secret statement to top Iraqi civilian and military leaders.

Only a couple of weeks ago people were laughing and making the vilest remarks. They said I was such a lackey and coward my wives had either barred me from our homes or at least withheld all reasonable marital prerogatives. This was justified, the ruffians said, since I had asked my presumed-close-friend-and-eternal-ally President George W. Bush to swear he would not summarily yank American troops from Iraq and thus leave me like a plump turkey in the clutches of potentially any of many ravenous sects, militias, and political discussion groups.

Actually, I'm glad the enemies of democracy distorted and lied and thus spurred me to immediately order what I'd been religiously planning and would have soon done anyway: I demanded all American troops cease blockading Baghdad streets. They were causing traffic jams, and manhandling, searching, and sometimes even fondling our citizens, many of whom were veiled females. One soldier, who will surely face capital charges, was seen lifting ebony cloth and kissing a lady, who we then had to arrest and reprogram.

As my elite troops and security forces moved into forward positions, the Americans scurried to pull back and disappear. This was their fastest retreat and most ignominious rout since hundreds of thousands of Chinese soldiers rolled south across the Yalu River and almost pushed the Americans off the Korean Peninsula into the sea. I was exhilarated and for the first time foresaw I am destined not to be America's puppet but its conqueror.

Accordingly, I have resolved to exploit the historical initiative I created. One week from today I shall order all American troops off Iraqi soil. They can go to the moon. They can go home. But they can't stay here. Surely they won't try to. They've sworn they're here to build a strong and free democratic government. And they have. Our sovereign nation demands its sovereignty.

If Iraq is not free of occupying troops within two months, the infidels will be first ensnared then crushed by my strategic masterwork. We will strike them with weapons of mass destruction. Yes, we have them well-hidden and ready to confound an enemy soon to be doubly disheartened by the specter of a just-freed Saddam mounted on a white stallion and armed with a saber. He will rally the Sunnis as I arouse the Shiites, a groundswell that'll compel the whole Muslim world to arm and embrace us. Russia, currently being encircled again in Cold War style, will surely join us, and so will China, which is terrified of U.S. naval might in the Pacific. Our grand alliance will defeat the enemy and secure our homelands. And I shall emerge as the ultimate earthly leader and put Saddam back in prison if he hasn't already fallen in battle.

Bush Embraces the New Political World

I didn't see this coming. You might ask how I missed it since polls indicated a significant political shift was probable. Well, I guess I feared it but didn't think it would actually happen. I've been on a special mission and just couldn't see it derailed. And I'm not saying things are off track. I'm a positive guy. Why all the glum faces? Look at my mug. I'm smiling. It's not my happiest smile but that's okay. I congratulate the Democrats on winning enough midterm elections to become the majority party in both the Senate and House of Representatives. That's great. We can work together and wrestle through our differences. That's what democracy is all about. We had an even better democracy before, but now it's about negotiation and compromise.

I'm delighted Nancy Pelosi will be the new Speaker of the House of Representatives. She's called me a dangerous and incompetent liar and an emperor with no clothes, and she favors more stem cell research and reducing my tax cuts for the wealthy and increasing the minimum wage – all scary stuff – but I'll deal with it. I've got to. And I'm not afraid to. I've been through lots of campaigns, my own and my dad's, and almost all of them were victorious. I can take a rare loss. It's not really my loss. Other Republicans lost, but as leader of the party I realize some of the responsibility is mine. I accept it. I love responsibility. That's why I've done so much to minimize the influence of others.

That's over. I worked in a bipartisan way as Governor of Texas, and I told Nancy – we're not using first names yet, but will be – the other day at lunch that she may not agree this narrow Democratic victory is a victory for terrorists, since the Demos believe in waiting to be attacked, but we both love America equally and therefore have the same ultimate goals we've being pursuing in different ways that are sure to become more alike.

There'll be some changes at the Department of Defense, and that surprised the heck out of me. I had no idea I was going to ask for the resignation of Pentagon boss Donald Rumsfeld, a military mastermind so profound he often degraded top generals. Actually, I didn't ask him to step down. He offered to. You know that. He'd done so at least twice after my reelection. He didn't want to be a political liability. And as long as we had both branches of congress and a majority of the citizens, he wasn't. He is now, so like a good soldier he's pouncing on the grenade, knowing we need fresh eyes on Iraq.

Two of those eyes belong to Robert Gates, who was director of the CIA for my dad and is a key member of the bipartisan Iraq Study Group that's going to give me advice that I hadn't wanted but will have to listen to. It's great Gates is now my guy. I suppose he's really more my dad's guy. My dad and Gates and Colin Powell, who I axed as Secretary of State because he wasn't aggressive enough, were also meek and shortsighted back in 1991 during Desert Storm when they had the opportunity to ignore the limited United Nations mandate, to only liberate Kuwait from the Iraqis, and instead go all the way into Baghdad and oust Saddam to free Iraq. They claimed that would have caused all kinds of sectarian violence and civilian deaths and occupation problems, and I wasn't listening to that crap, even from my dad.

I'm listening now. But I'm still not listening all that much. Instead, I keep saying – and never get tired of it – that in order to protect the American people from attack I've got to help the Iraqis defend themselves against Al Qaeda and other terrorists who didn't exist in Iraq before I invaded and severely increased the problem. I know it's a tough fight. War is tough. My dad told me that and so did the families of dead soldiers I often commiserate with. It's tough talking to them but I know they know the only way we can lose the war is to come home before the job is done. And if we did that, the terrorists would follow us home. So I say to our enemies: that's not going to happen. This isn't another Vietnam. We've had democratic elections in Iraq, we've got a volunteer army nowadays, and, unlike the Vietnamese, the Iraqis aren't having a civil war. It's something else, even though they're killing each other by the tens of thousands, and that distinction is real important, and I promise that as long as I'm president whatever happens in Iraq will never be called a civil war.

2007

CHAPTER 5

Saddam Hussein's Final Interview

Eleven days ago in a darkened room cold before dawn Saddam Hussein stood hoodless and neck-tied on the gallows as former subjects taunted and filmed him until the trapdoor snapped. Soon thereafter he was received by The Gatekeeper. A transcript of their exchange follows.

The Gatekeeper – We must put the sharp pieces of your life together. Though this in no way mitigates your actions as an adult, you did have a remarkably difficult beginning in the world.

Saddam Hussein – My father died when my mother was pregnant then my brother perished and my mother tried first to abort me then kill herself before I could be born. Later, she was too bereaved to care and I was thrown to my Uncle Khairalla who was imprisoned after a coup attempt which hurled me back to my mother whose new husband beat me.

TG – In 1958, at age 21, your Uncle Khairalla ordered you to murder a communist.

SH – I didn't murder him. I put a bullet through his skull during our battle for independence. There was no criminal evidence against me, and I was released after six months in prison.

TG – You then married your uncle's daughter, Dajida, your first cousin.

SH – We created two heroic sons, Uday and Qusay, as well as three lovely daughters.

TG – In 1959 General Bakr, your cousin and one of the Baath Party leaders, ordered you and others to assassinate Iraq's leader, Brigadier Abdul Karim Qasim.

SH – We failed and only wounded the traitor. I was shot in the leg but escaped to Syria then Egypt. The illegitimate government sentenced me to death in absentia in 1960. Meanwhile, after a late start in formal education, I finished my secondary school studies. I was reading and learning more about the Western criminals who'd long been crushing us. In 1961 the British, who should never have entered Arab territory, decided Kuwait would be independent despite for millennia having been part of Mesopotamia, from which Iraq had been artificially formed.

Naturally, I began to study and admire Stalin. He knew how to deal with the West and all other enemies external and internal. Like Khrushchev said, "Stalin was an overpowering personality." I began to see this quality in myself. And so did many others.

Back in Iraq in 1963, I was studying at Baghdad Law College and involved in activities of the Baath Party, which had taken power. A coup soon forced me to rush back into exile but I often returned undercover and worked for freedom until being arrested in October 1964. In prison I became one of the leaders of the Baath Party. My cousin made me his deputy, and after escaping from prison in 1967 I took over Baath security and was instrumental the following year in our return to power. Our leadership was dominated by the best and most loyal men, most of them fellow Sunnis from my hometown Tikrit. As chairman of the Revolutionary Command Council, I was urged by my cousin, the new President Bakr, to rid the government of dangerous enemies. After they tried to overthrow us, I intensified the purges. My power increased as I assumed command of internal security and the Iraqi Atomic Energy Commission. The nation respected me all the more in 1969 when I ordered the public hanging of 11 Iraqis who'd been spying for Israel, which since the Six Day War in 1967 had been occupying sacred Arab land.

TG – You say the nation respected you. Don't you mean feared?

SH – To be respected, a political leader must be feared. Fear ensures compliance. We guaranteed that by expanding our surveillance network, creating a militia, and keeping power concentrated with my cousin President Bakr, my brother-in-law General Talfah, and me.

TG – In 1970 the Iraqi government signed a "Manifesto" that promised to grant the Kurds "significant autonomy." That never happened.

SH – The Kurds were hostile. They…

TG – We'll talk more about them later. In the early and mid-1970's you received a law degree and were promoted first to lieutenant-general then general. Do you really believe you were qualified in either profession?

SH – Absolutely. I was the supreme law of the land, and the supreme commander in war.

TG – That's my point. Your competence in those areas was quite limited. Let's move on. Iraq began to develop chemical weapons and signed the 15-Year Treaty of Friendship and Cooperation with the Soviet Union, which provided billions of dollars of weapons and training. France soon became your second largest arms supplier, and in fact sold Iraq a nuclear reactor.

SH – The Zionists destroyed that several years later.

TG – Correct. And well before that, in 1974, rather than grant the Kurds self-rule, as promised, the Baathists signed an agreement with the Shah of Iran that led to his destroying all Kurdish villages along an 800-mile stretch of the Iranian border with Iraq.

SH – All necessary moves. But let me point out, for your edification, that for a generation my domestic programs were exceptional: industrial production soared; health care improved; and education flourished as I mandated literacy for all citizens and enforced attendance with three-year prison sentences

TG – And in 1976 you evidently advanced your own education when you received a master's degree in military science.

SH – I was preparing for war on many fronts. Throughout the Middle East, Arabs looked to me for guidance and strength, especially after I denounced President Sadat and Egypt for accepting the return of the Sinai in exchange for peace with Israel.

TG – Don't you think both countries made a wise and noble move?

SH – No. The Palestinians were betrayed. Palestine is for Arabs.

TG – The real world is more complicated than that. In 1979 you tried to simplify everything by inviting the Revolutionary Command Council and hundreds of Baathist officials to a conference where you casually smoked while name after name was called, and shocked and frightened men, many who'd thought they were in good standing, got up and disappeared.

SH – Most of the traitors didn't disappear. They died in public. That delighted the Iraqi people who approved as I was named, among many titles, president, field marshal, and commander-in-chief of the armed forces.

TG – What happened to President Bakr, your trusting cousin?

SH – He got too old to serve in high office, and he resigned.

TG – Many say he died mysteriously.

SH – No mystery. He was ill. I'd been in control, anyway. The people needed one strong man to be wary of the Russians after their invasion of Afghanistan, to crush Iraqi Shias who tried to kill members of my cabinet, to send Shias of Iranian origin back to that Khomeini-crazed country, and, ultimately, to invade Iran.

TG – Without irony I must say that you should've studied harder in military school. The Iran-Iraq war was eight years of unmitigated slaughter. Hundreds of thousands died on each side.

SH – We killed twice as many of them. The United States understood the danger Iran posed, and still poses. We never seized a U.S. Embassy. The Americans helped us with credits to buy their agricultural products, which included such flexible items as chemical analysis equipment and "bacteria-fungi-protozoa that could be used to manufacture biological weapons, like anthrax." Owing in part to this assistance, I was able to eliminate thousands of Kurdish rebels.

In 1982, after two years of fighting, I wanted peace with Iran but the fanatics suicidally attacked us, in human waves, trying to annihilate our entire nation. Thankfully, my military leadership and Soviet weapons enabled us to contain them.

The Americans were also very helpful. Donald Rumsfeld came to Iraq in December 1983 and emphasized America's eagerness to resume "full diplomatic relations" and thereby acquire a powerful anti-Iranian ally and one which not only battled that colossus but gassed several thousand more Kurds and executed many treacherous Shias in Iraq. In March 1984 Rumsfeld returned to Baghdad, and the very day he met with my foreign minister the United Nations released a report that Iraq was killing Iranian attackers with "mustard gas and the nerve agent tabun." It's devastating to note that three weeks before Rumseld's arrival, the Americans had released this statement: "Available evidence indicates Iraq has used lethal chemical weapons."

The Americans soon rewarded me with a full diplomatic embrace and military assistance that included "battle-planning, detailed information on Iranian deployments, plans for air strikes, satellite

photographs of the war front, and bomb-damage assessments."
 Our American allies didn't give a damn about gas.

TG – During this period, four thousand Iraqi prisoners were executed at Abu Ghraib prison.

SH – Don't tell me about Abu Ghraib.

TG – Don't compare sexual degradation, lamentable though it is, with mass murder. And by the way, you were by then killing scores of thousands of Kurds and destroying hundreds of their villages.

SH – I could not have done so without the Americans. Several years later, in 1994, a United States Senate committee reported that "from 1985 to 1989 pathogenic, toxigenic, and other biological research materials were shipped to Iraq by US firms and that the exports were approved and licensed by the U.S. Department of Commerce, with shipments continuing up to November 1989."

TG – Imagine how immeasurably better things would have been if you'd become a man of peace when the war with Iran ended in August 1988.

SH – Peace would have been impossible. I had to rebuild the army and produce biological agents.

TG – Why?

SH – To deter the Iranians and Israelis, and to deal with the Kuwaitis, who were driving down oil prices by overproducing. I told them that undercut our struggling economy. They didn't care. No, they continued siphoning oil from a vast field partly in Iraq. I was forced to invade Kuwait in August 1990.

It shocked me when my American friends demanded I withdraw. But I knew, based on their defeat in Viet Nam, that they were weaklings who would shrivel in the desert if they attacked us.

TG – Thirty-three alarmed nations, several of them Arab, formed a coalition against you, and you were crushed. At least a hundred thousand of your soldiers died along with several thousand citizens. You had to unconditionally agree to destroy all your weapons of mass destruction and face economic sanctions until you did so.

SH – I destroyed the weapons of mass destruction, just as I later said, didn't I?

TG – Yes, apparently so, but not all of them until after the 1995 defection of your two sons-in-law who revealed you'd imported about 40 tons of "growth media for biological agents." Then you killed the men after they'd been promised a safe return to Iraq.

SH – I didn't kill them. Outraged relatives exacted revenge for their treachery, "purifying and healing the family by amputating an ailing finger from the hand."

TG – In the late 1990's you appeared to be hiding weapons in dozens of "restricted presidential sites" that you had, in writing, agreed to open up for United Nations inspectors. Instead, in 1998 your intransigence forced the inspectors to leave Iraq.

SH – Their job had been completed.

TG – Then you should have more energetically permitted them to verify that. You might not have been brought to justice.

SH – Those on trial should be Americans and others who choked our devastated country with sanctions and were responsible for the deaths of tens of thousands of our children. The Red Cross correctly reported there was a "catastrophic breakdown of the health system, hygiene, and water supply in Iraq." Yet, what did we get? Sanctions. Always more sanctions.

TG – Your professed concern for the children of Iraq is belied by your squandering billions of dollars of oil revenues on palaces and other unjustifiable luxuries.

Furthermore, your mental state, which has always worried many, was gravely questioned on the 10th anniversary of the invasion of Kuwait when you announced Iraq had won the Gulf War.

SH – It was a political victory. My popularity had risen while that of the United States, as we've seen, would decline.

TG – U.S. popularity has certainly declined in the Middle East and elsewhere during the administration of George W. Bush, but you have long had so few friends and too many enemies.

SH – I should've had more friends outside Iraq. Then Bush couldn't have framed me.

TG – You kept hedging when required to yield unconditional access to potential weapons sites. Again, you denied unrestricted entry to "42 presidential sites."

SH – I thought Americans believed innocent until proven guilty.

TG – It was rather the opposite in this case, and you should've realized that.

SH – I did, eventually. Like everyone I'd heard Bush's rants for preemptive war and unilateral strikes and regime change in Iraq. In September 2002 he said he wanted me prosecuted for war crimes. I here demand that George W. Bush be prosecuted for the deaths, intended or not, of some 50,000 Iraqi civilians who'd be breathing today were it not for his unjustifiable attack on an unthreatening, sovereign nation.

We accepted the American terms. The United Nations Monitoring, Verification and Inspection Commission was granted full access. They found no evidence, but Bush continued his imperialist buildup in my backyard, so I offered "to permit U.S. troops to enter the country to look for weapons of mass destruction and to prove that Iraq was not involved in the September 11 attacks." This offer was rejected. Bush was behaving like the schoolyard bully who slugs you harder the nicer you treat him.

Notice he hasn't attacked North Korea, a nation that is decidedly defiant and well-armed. George W. Bush is a coward who'll someday have plenty of bloody questions to answer.

TG – He had nothing to do with all your many aforementioned atrocities.

SH – They were legitimate and lawful acts of self-defense by an independent nation.

TG – You went way beyond that, and the world knows that and so do Iraqis and somewhere inside you also know. No man kills that many people with a completely untroubled conscience.

You still could have saved yourself. President Bush gave you and your sons 48 hours to get out of the country.

SH – I give him 48 hours to go to hell. Look at the polls. The majority of Iraqis view American troops not as liberators but as occupiers since 2003, and want them to leave immediately.

Dick Cheney infamously claimed "the insurgency is in its last throes." Strange, isn't it? Twice as many civilians were killed in year two of the occupation than in the first year. And more than a hundred American soldiers died in Iraq in December 2006. Bush and Cheney have wrought a catastrophe.

TG – In fairness, we should note that Iraqi criminals and insurgents killed more civilians than the United States.

SH – Criminals and insurgents wouldn't have been killing anyone if I'd remained in power.

TG – You'd have been killing people.

SH – Not nearly as many.

TG – Your record indicates the bloodshed would have been comparable.

SH – Need for bloodshed had waned. The Americans had us in a vise, with no-fly zones in our north and south and eternal economic sanctions shoved down our starving throats.

Furthermore, all credible American and international investigations have proved the obvious: I detested Osama bin Laden and Al Qaeda, and considered them a threat to my regime and to secular governments in general.

TG – Granted, you weren't helping bin Laden. But you were convicted of killing 148 people in the village of Dujail in July 1982.

SH – Every commander-in-chief must strike those who try to kill him. There was a conspiracy to overthrow the rightful government of Iraq. I believe, based on information, that most of those executed were involved. Is it possible some innocent people were killed? Let me ask you: is it possible some innocent men suspected of terrorism have long been held in silence by the United States?

TG – Do you feel you got a fair trial?

SH – Three of my lawyers have been murdered. Is that fair? And I was tortured in my box-like cell by American captors.

TG – I don't believe you were tortured.

SH – Look at the Abu Ghraib atrocities.

TG – I'm talking about you. What physical evidence of torture was documented?

SH – They wouldn't have documented it. They let me heal. I countered by going on hunger strikes. I wasn't the aggressor. Bush was

TG – Until recently you were also on trial for killing as many as 100,000 Kurds during the Anful campaign of 1987-88.

SH – I wanted to defend myself. I had much to say.

TG – I think the world was tired of your voice.

SH – Then I will say only what Hermann Goering did at Nuremberg: "The victor will always be the accuser, and the vanquished the accused."

TG – You handled yourself with dignity on the gallows.

SH – The duty of a martyr whose popularity is surging.

TG – Welcome, Saddam Hussein.

SH – Will I at last be with God?

TG – You'll be the same place as everyone else who heads this way.

President Bush Explains the Surge

It doesn't matter what you think. Only what I want matters. And I want a surge. Iraq's got to have it. It'll make all the difference. We can't win unless we send twenty thousand more troops into Baghdad. We won't do it all at once, of course. We'll only push soldiers in fast as we can find them. Some may be reluctant. Despite my nonstop proclamations, many people don't understand the struggle in Iraq will determine the course of the global war on terrorism. If we fail in Baghdad, it would be a disaster for United States security just like our losing Saigon damn near destroyed us and the rest of the world.

I'm not going to let that happen. I've learned from my blunders. Last year I thought twelve million Iraqis voting in an open democratic election proved they were coming together and their U.S.-trained security forces could keep them pacified and happy. My strategy would've worked, too, if Al Qaeda and Sunni terrorists hadn't destroyed the Shia's holy Golden Mosque of Samarra. This outrage inflamed Shias who formed death squads supported by Iran, which has no right to influence events in neighboring countries. I'll decide what happens in places bordering Iran.

We are not going to permit radicalism and sectarian violence to overwhelm the Middle East and enable terrorists to gain strength and recruits, and steal oil revenues to finance their jihad to destroy our way of life, and embolden Iran to become a nuclear powerhouse. Our task, though critical, is remarkably easy to spot on a map: eighty percent of sectarian violence takes place within thirty miles of Baghdad. We stamp that out and unify the fractured capital city, and I guarantee Muslims worldwide will behave as I want them to.

I'm confident because of my instincts about what's right for other people. We would've already taken care of their needs but for two small errors: we didn't have enough American and Iraqi troops to secure neighborhoods and there were too many restrictions on those too-few troops. Well, we're taking off the gloves and appointing three Iraqi commanders for Baghdad and we're deploying Iraqi Army and National Police brigades, deeply embedded with my new American strike forces, across the nine districts of the capital. We'll gain the trust of Iraqi citizens by more often stopping and frisking them at checkpoints, conducting patrols, and knocking on their doors at all hours.

This time, I promise you, we won't leave newly-secured neighborhoods to be recaptured by terrorists. We can stay since we'll have the necessary force levels and the green light to neutralize as many people as we think necessary. Prime Minister Maliki also promises not to tolerate political and sectarian violence. And I believe him even though he's close to and supported by Moqtada al-Sadr and his Shia death squads, which are as bad as anything Saddam had. Don't worry. Maliki is still our guy. Saddam was once our guy, too. But that changed, and look what happened to him. Maliki won't go that way.

Prime Minister Maliki and other Iraqi leaders understand America's commitment is not absolute. If the Iraqis don't keep their promises, the American people will not support them. And they wouldn't tolerate me anymore, either. Americans just need to be patient and understand my new strategy won't immediately end the nightmare. Our enemies need violence to survive, and they will seek it. Nevertheless, we will eventually see Iraqi troops apprehending murderers, reducing crime, and earning the trust of Baghdadis. When this great day arrives, the government and the people will have a peaceful and stable nation.

Keep in mind, these developments will never happen unless twenty thousand more American troops are deployed in Baghdad. Without them – and the reconstruction, self-reliance, and reconciliation they'll bring – we will inevitably face an Islamic Empire led by Al Qaeda.

Thank God even my enemies in America acknowledge that in our enlightened democratic system there really is no way to deny me more troops. I can make war when and where I want. There have been some meows about Democrats and a few weak Republicans denying me funding for more troops. But if they do that, I'll accuse them of helping Iran and Syria, and abandoning our troops, and undermining American interests, which only I completely understand and am qualified to protect.

Our challenges in the Middle East are the decisive ideological struggle of our time. We must ensure the survival of the young Iraqi democracy as well as the monarchs I hold hands with in Saudi Arabia.

If we fail to demand of ourselves more patience, sacrifice, and resolve, then unimaginable mass killing will be inevitable. That won't happen on my watch.

White House Statements on Proper Deaths

For Immediate Release:

The White House is distraught about the recent unsightly and quite unintentional decapitation of Saddam Hussein's half-brother, Barzan Ibrahim al-Tikriti. We have already rebuked Iraqi political officials and ordered them to follow our rules of expert and (almost) immaculate execution.

In regard to hanging the murderous half-brother, a simple review of the 1947 U.S. Army manual on executions would have precluded all problems. The chart on page nine is a model of scientific clarity, listing a man's weight and the corresponding drop necessary to snap his neck. If a man weighs 120-130 pounds, drop him about eight feet. A 140-pounder needs to fall some seven feet. For 170-pounders, like Ibrahim, a six-foot journey will suffice. A man more than 200 pounds has to travel but five feet to eternity. Drop him too little, and he gags and chokes in the noose and might have to be finished by other means. Drop him too far, as we witnessed in Ibrahim's eight-foot plunge, and his head will be ripped off and roll away from a blood-gushing body. Thankfully, Ibrahim's head was in a hood. Imagine if Saddam's hoodless head had been bouncing around.

If the Iraqis botch another hanging, the United States will have to take over. And that would be for the best. As in many states, the military now mandates death by lethal injection. This technique is both subtle and humane. According to the U.S. Army Procedures for Executions, updated in January 2006, a killer receives a dignified entrance on a gurney and the careful insertion of a "large-bore intravenous channel into an appropriate vein." At that point the condemned man is serenaded by the commander reading charges and sentence prior to administration of "lethal agents" after which his death will be verified by an electrocardiograph machine, not the groping hands of enemies.

Even though many Iraqis who will be put to death have gassed innocent civilians, the White House does not wish to see the former group executed in gas chambers. Prisoners there often try to hold their breath until they inevitably inhale noxious fumes that make them gag, grimace, and groan before they expire. That is most primitive. So is the electric chair. A man should not have to be shorn of his locks in order to die. And we do not like the vulgarity of a sparky procedure which burns the condemned and forces final grimaces that frequently upset some witnesses.

Death is an important issue in Iraq, and the White House has certainly been proactive in that regard. Though our military no longer uses musketry to execute heinous criminals, we do kill thousands of people that way and so do our friends and enemies – who are often the same – in Iraq. The essential difference: the Iraqis are untidy. To better themselves in that regard, they should again refer to the 1947 U.S. Army manual which mandates those condemned – as the Shiites and Sunnis daily condemn each other – receive a formal escort, sometimes including a band, to the place of execution where a shiny ambulance is ready to take the decedent away. We don't toss (often headless) corpses into rivers, sewers or dumps. With three thousand Iraqi civilians a month dying violently, there is already sufficient psychological horror and hygienic distress.

As often as possible, we keep things surgically clean by destroying the enemy from afar with fantastically-expensive technology. They counter by using crude bombs to kill other Iraqis as well as our uniformed soldiers traveling in convenient convoys. What we do is noble. What they do is ignoble. That is the position of this White House.

Bush Resolves Missile Shield Dilemma

I would've thought President Putin of Russia understood that my proposed ABM (anti ballistic missile) shield in the Czech Republic and Poland was in no way aimed next door at his country. Geometry and geography prove the system would really be designed to intercept nuclear missiles fired from rogue states like Iran. I was shocked when Vladimir – I like calling him that – said my move would cause a resumption of the Cold War and provoke another missile race. We beat those guys in the last Cold War and could certainly do so again, but that stuff can get dangerous and expensive, and our allies wouldn't like it and neither would I.

I felt a lot better when Vladimir said, "George, let's join forces, as our two great nations did during World War II. I'll let you use our antiquated radar systems in Azerbaijan and you, and perhaps we, could shoot down incoming missiles with our own missiles fired from cruisers."

I'm a little worried about that because I don't think sea-based ABMs would be as dependable as those based on land, and, let's face it, those on land are still damned undependable. I shouldn't say this publicly, and don't often admit it to myself, but right now those ABMs couldn't shoot down a goose much less a missile. Not only that, the Azeris are only leasing the facilities to the Russians and have already started howling in resistance to such a defensive system being based on their territory. I suppose we could attack them and get bases that way, but Vladimir came up with even better ideas.

"Let's put the ABMs in Iraq and Turkey," he said. "You've been fighting terrorists in Iraq, anyway, and Turkey's your long-time NATO ally."

Right away the Iraqis complained about the idea, hollering they hadn't even been consulted and didn't want to do it. And the Turks weren't too positive either. That's when I had a vision that'll soon be overwhelming as my doctrine of invade to democratize.

Let's start with Russia. No, if Vladimir hears his country first he'll get KGB-style paranoid. We can begin right here at home and erect

ABM batteries around all our ICBM (intercontinental ballistic missile) sites and really protect them. The Russians would also encircle their offensive missiles with defensive missiles and so would all other nations that have, or soon will have, nuclear-armed missiles. I'm sure France and Great Britain would jump on board. China, India, Pakistan, and Israel probably would too. With that kind of powerful alliance, Iran and North Korea would have to go along.

Now, I know what my critics are saying. I'm the one who caused this whole commotion by tearing up the ABM Treaty that had long ensured deterrence by forcing Russia and the United States to accept any nuclear attack would lead nowhere except MAD (Mutually Assured Destruction.)

How dare George W. Bush throw all that away, my enemies fumed? They didn't know I'd come up with such an extraordinary plan. And the unbelievable part is this: all those ABMs would be targeted against their own offensive missiles. How 'bout that?

Saddam Gloats over Iraqi Chaos

Who wrote that headline? I'm not gloating. I'm traumatized that six months after hanging me the Americans are still ravaging my country. Everyone knows scores (if not hundreds) of thousands of Iraqi civilians have died since the apocalyptic United States invasion in April 2003. Now the occupiers are testifying they will need to stay here "many years" more. Let me use a phrase I picked up in captivity: what the hell for?

Oh, yes, I know, there are many profound strategic reasons, the most urgent being to protect Iraq and the rest of the Arab-oil world from Iranian domination if not outright occupation. I will ask a simple rhetorical question and if you say yes then I'll know you're a liar: when I ruled was there any danger that Iran would overwhelm Iraq or any other Arab nation? Certainly not – I killed almost a million Iranians, gassed them, shot them, blew them up. Supported by the United States, I served as what the Washington think tank boys called an "invaluable counterweight" to Persian expansion.

George W. Bush and his clique, having mangled the most critical strategic issue, desperately need you to at least hope that average Iraqis are safer and more content now that my bloodthirsty soul has been removed from the corporeal world. Iraqis may at times be pleased about my physical absence, but they increasingly crave my authoritative return as they're being tortured, wounded or killed. The mighty American forces are far more adroit at eliminating Iraqis than protecting them. And I profoundly understand the violent paranoia of a tyrant under siege. The U.S. death total in May 2007 was its third highest of the war, and overall 3,500 invaders have been killed and 26,000 wounded, many catastrophically. The Americans have to be wondering: what the hell for?

Why don't the anti-genocide champions of democracy rescue Darfur? I suppose it reminds them of Rwanda. They're more comfortable building nations on vast petroleum reserves. We all know that. But until last week we hadn't heard such succinct and devastating figures about the failure to secure Iraq. I shall start with an Iraqi Army besieged by permanent absentee rates of 25 percent, eternal infiltration by Jihadists – can you imagine that in my army? – and incompetent military performance. The current Iraqi Army is delighted to lose only 18 percent of its soldiers annually to death, injury, or desertion, and celebrates when half a combat unit deigns to come to work. The police have similar problems. They've lost almost a fifth of their men in the last year and a half. About half of those are dead and many of the others are "unaccounted for." Plenty of them, as well as the invisible soldiers, are Jihadists fighting the Americans, many of whom believe about half their comrades in arms are insurgents.

I must therefore ask the Americans: are you sure you're going to stay many more years?

Consequences of Defeat in Iraq

If we don't cut and run like the liberals and a few traitorous Republican senators want us to, we can still win in Iraq and we must do so for our children and grandchildren. The consequences of a complete withdrawal of United States troops would be catastrophic. I can see it better than you because I'm your commander-in-chief but soon you'll also understand that before the last American left Al Qaeda would have taken over the country and established a terrorist base from which it would ceaselessly attack the United States. In such a lawless Iraq the semi-autonomous Kurds in the north would join with Turkish Kurds and start a war with thousands of Turkish troops already grinding their teeth on the Iraqi border. At that point the Iranians, using the increasing belligerence of their Kurds as a pretext to attack, would charge into chaotic Iraq and embrace the terrorists.

Meanwhile, without our forces in Afghanistan, Al Qaeda and the Taliban would regain control there, and incite fellow Jihadists in Pakistan to overthrow President Musharraf. At that point there'd be an unbroken Axis of Evil from Pakistan to Afghanistan through Iran to Iraq. And you know that kind of mayhem would embolden Hamas, after its bloody victory in Gaza, to try to devour the West Bank. The Israelis would respond with such overwhelming might their defenses would be weakened near Lebanon where Hezbollah would start launching missiles and luring Israeli troops into a trap they'd spring with their allies the Syrians, who'd also go after the Golan Heights.

In such a crazed Middle East, Jihadists in Egypt could not be stopped from overthrowing President Mubarak and mobilizing massive forces against the Israelis in Gaza and the Sinai. King Abdullah of Jordan would then act like his father, King Hussein, in 1967, and try to annihilate Israel which would threaten to respond with nuclear weapons. And all those threats would inevitably bring us back in far greater numbers than ever, and we'd be tied down in every place I've mentioned, and to do that we'd have to bring back the draft which would rouse the Russians and Chinese and Indians to align themselves against us.

And that is why we must stay the course in Iraq and will as long as I'm president.

Boehner Rebukes Republicans

I am intrepid. I have to be. As House Majority Leader I, John Boehner, must prove no one in the world is remotely as tough and resolute as pro-war Republicans. Until recently all Republicans wanted war. That solidarity both gratified and emboldened us to try to remake the world in our image. Now our great task is imperiled not merely by Democrats and other liberals but even a handful from my sacred party who are thinking independently and concluding that the troop trickle in Iraq is a failure and should be redressed by prompt withdrawal of some of our military personnel. I recently called such Republicans wimps.

That's what they are. Check the conservative blogs. You'll see I'm right. Patriots are writing in that the wimps are also traitors and worse. And Democrats are already targeting them for electoral defeat next year. Instead of sacrificing their political careers to maintain U.S. military operations in Iraq, these Republicans are behaving as our opponents and "sheepishly dismissing the challenges of a post 9/11 world."

Our task is unequivocal: we must stay and support the Iraqis until their security forces are ready, whether that process takes five, 10, or even 100 years. If we do less, we will die. I understand that. Like President Bush and Vice President Cheney, I have a profound feel for security issues. I signed up for the navy in 1968 and doubtless would have killed many communist Vietnamese – who, like the Iraqis, were trying to conquer the world – but I had to leave the armed forces after two months training because I had a bad back. Can you imagine? Some guys called me a wimp.

The people in my Ohio district between Dayton and Cincinnati know what I'm really like, and they've elected me nine times. They love it when I stand up for what I believe. On the august floor of the House of Representatives, in 1995, I boldly strode back and forth, delivering "campaign contributions from tobacco industry lobbyists" while my colleagues were considering "how to vote on tobacco subsidies." To do that, you've got to have balls.

Osama bin Laden to Sue Al Qaeda Franchises

I do not live in a cave most of the time. That isn't necessary since the Americans have been reluctant to invade my haven in the north-western wilds of Pakistan. They know such aggression would compel Pakistanis, who love vigorous Islam and loathe the West, to eliminate their imperialist ally, President Musharraf, and launch themselves into my embrace. Then we'd have a real Al Qaeda nation with me as at least the de facto leader.

It is essential that I be in charge, and in particular mandatory I maintain control of any group calling itself Al Qaeda. I have been much too tolerant in permitting scores of paramilitary entities, and sometimes mere debating clubs, to use my internationally feared and respected brand name. Effective at once, I'm going to sue those who without authorization pretend to be Al Qaeda and thus architects of grand strategy and new world order.

I've already hired several law firms around the globe, and litigation is being prepared. Some have asked why I didn't do this earlier. First, in order to maintain my unique skills and unshakable commitment to the destruction of our enemies, I had to survive, and that meant hiding all the time, moving often, and not doing any real military planning and instead being satisfied occasionally making videos. Some callow and insignificant Jihadists began implying I was more interested in urging others to martyr themselves than becoming one myself. For that reason I was delighted when Abu Musab al-Zarqawi proclaimed himself the leader of Al Qaeda in Iraq. I praised him, not in public of course, but publicly on audio tape. He was a crude fellow, personally decapitating people and such, but he soothed my radical critics and absorbed much of the hot pursuit by the United States. Indeed, five times a day I pray the Americans will not leave Iraq for when they do anyone calling himself Al Qaeda is likely to be dismembered by ungrateful militias.

Since I am still the unrivalled spiritual leader of Jihad, and the only one who can provide political and military leadership of historical dimension, the dozens of self-proclaimed Al Qaeda cells in Iraq and elsewhere in the Middle East, including Turkey, and in the Philippines and Indonesia, and in Western abscesses Spain, England and Germany, and indeed in most of Europe, will have to pay for the use of a special name just as you would if you opened a restaurant called McDonald's. The franchise fee I'm charging depends on the size and assets of the cell. In general terms I demand about five hundred thousand dollars from a group with more gall than gold, and at least two million from those blessed and cursed to come from aristocratic backgrounds such as my own.

Where do you send the checks? Before long I think they'll go to the new President of Pakistan.

Grand Speeches

I just slapped on my morning lather and slid a sharp new blade into the razor and, admiring my smug mug, am thinking about my recent speeches of such strategic importance. I love what my speechwriters give me because they've written the feelings and visions of the world's most important man and a guy who I'm confident history will prove was right about the transformative power of unprovoked aggression.

A man with my meager martial record has got to be special to walk in front of a hall full of warriors at the convention of the Veteran's of Foreign War, as I did on August twenty-second, and declare that I stood before them a wartime president and was proud to be their commander-in-chief and leader of the greatest force for human liberation the world has ever known. We all instinctively understand, even my domestic adversaries, that He has chosen me for the supreme task of struggling for civilization against barbarians who slaughtered thousands on United States soil and seek to kill millions.

We had an enemy who sneak attacked us because he despised freedom, used suicide bombers, and tried to dominate an entire region and the world. I'm not talking about Al Qaeda. I'm referring to Imperial Japan. Our permanent troop deployments there after World War II, as well as in Korea following that war, enabled those Asian nations to become free and prosperous and a model for others in the area. We stayed despite countless critics insisting we were foolish to bleed while trying to help people who never would understand freedom.

Everyone understands freedom. That's why we made a bloody error in abandoning the Vietnamese. I wish I'd been there. I'd have stayed because I knew withdrawal would lead to millions of deaths in the region, especially in neighboring Cambodia. That's exactly what would happen if we betrayed Iraq. Don't listen to liberals and other non-warriors who say U.S. intervention and the secret bombing campaign destabilized Cambodia and precipitated the slaughter by Pol Pot. Don't pay attention to claims that the victorious communist Vietnamese were the ones who invaded to remove Pol Pot. And above all tune out observations – which damn few Democrats ever make anyway – that the United States killed about two million Southeast Asians, maimed many more, and dropped more bombs there than in all theaters during World War II. That stuff doesn't bother me or most Americans.

Our big worry now is that Osama bin Laden expects us to cut and run as we did then. He knows that Iraq is the central front of the war on terror. If it isn't, history will hang me in effigy. I won't permit that, and I'll never acknowledge there were no nukes and no Al Qaeda in the Iraq of Saddam Hussein. Why should I? I've liberated the fifty million citizens of Iraq and Afghanistan, and now they've learned "there's no power like the power of freedom."

No one can claim I'm not relentless. Only six days after the VFW speech, I strutted in front of the American Legion's national convention and asserted we always enter wars reluctantly. I did everything to avoid attacking Iraq, didn't I? But we had to attack because the "cradle of civilization became the home of the suicide bomber." The Sunnis want to impose their dark ideology "by raising up a violent and radical caliphate that spans from Spain to Indonesia."

But believe me, that's small potatoes compared to what Shiite Iranians are doing. They're backing Hezbollah, Hamas, the Palestinian Islamic Jihad, and the Taliban, and supplying sophisticated Improvised Explosive Devices to Iraqi terrorists and training them to "carry out attacks on our forces and the Iraqi people." Iran's Islamic Revolutionary Guard Corps is most responsible. Even though the IRGC is an official arm of the military, I've declared it a terrorist organization.

If not for Iranians, my policies in Iraq would have been even more successful, but now their "actions threaten the security of nations everywhere." And I see "what would happen if these forces of radicalism and extremism are allowed to drive us out of the Middle East. The region would be dramatically transformed in a way that could imperil the civilized world. Extremists of all strains would be emboldened by the knowledge they forced America to retreat. Terrorists could have safe havens to conduct attacks on America and our friends and allies. Iran could conclude that we were weak and unable to stop them from gaining nuclear weapons. And once Iran had nuclear weapons, it would set off a nuclear arms race in the region.

"Extremists would control a key part of the world's energy supply, and could blackmail and sabotage the global economy. They could use billions of dollars of oil revenues to buy weapons and pursue their deadly ambitions. Our allies in the region would be under greater siege by the enemies of freedom. Early movements toward democracy in the region would be violently reversed. This scenario would be a disaster for the people of the Middle East, a danger to our friends and allies, and a direct threat to American peace and security. This is what the extremists plan. For the sake of our own security, we'll pursue our enemies, we'll persevere and we will prevail."

Even for me, that's quite a barrage of threats and fear. I should relax a minute and be thankful we understand what history is demanding. We have momentum, thanks to The Surge. Look at Anbar Province. We thought we'd lost it to the terrorists. But now many "local Sunnis are turning against Al Qaeda...(and) are rejoining the political process... (In July) provincial officials reopened parts of the war-damaged government center with the help of one of our provincial reconstruction teams. Similar scenes are taking place all across Anbar."

I'm so damn excited by Anbar Province that I'm already wiping lather from my smooth face and am headed there now. Weren't those troops surprised when I popped in September third? They loved seeing their commander-in-chief. Look at that picture of me, left index finger pointed straight up as I lecture surrounding troops who either smile or gaze at me as if I were a rock star or Jesus Christ. I had this message: "For all the differences over the war, we can agree on what's working. And we can agree that continuing this progress is vital...in meeting the strategic interests of our nation. It's vital...that we work to bring America together behind a common vision for a more stable and more peaceful Middle East."

Pretty soon it's going to be vital for me to start proclaiming that the "central front on the war on terrorism" isn't really Iraq, it's Iran. And, by God, you know what that means.

Saddam Vows to Rescue Bush

To the American people I must first urgently say: don't worry. President George W. Bush, during one of many hazardous trips to Iraq, conferred with me in person and together we forcefully selected the most Saddam-like of my doubles and that dispensable fellow was the one who plummeted through the trapdoor into neck-snapped eternity. With astonishing foresight President Bush had decided to hold me in strategic reserve, secretly knowing that one day I might be the only one who could enable him to achieve his altruistic goals for my sacred homeland. That day is at hand, as the president and General David Petraeus have recently emphasized in many oblique and clever ways.

Now that I'm on the team I won't belabor that General Petraeus' optimistic reports before Congress about marginally improved security for Iraqi civilians reminds many Americans of the tragic miscalculations – or deceptions – by a succession of U.S. generals regarding progress in Viet Nam. The scholarly Professor Petraeus unfurled impressive charts and graphs to buttress his claim The Surge is working. Unfortunately, the free media in the West countered that even if some Iraqis are less likely to be shot or blown up, more American soldiers have been dying month by month than at the same time last year. And last week Sunnis shuddered after the somber Sheik Abu Risha, a U.S. ally who'd days before shaken hands with the gleeful Bush, was killed by an Al Qaeda bomb, becoming the ninth member of his family to fall fighting terrorists, who did not exist in the country when my hands encircled the national neck. Therefore, as benchmark number one, President Bush has ordered me to eliminate terrorism in Iraq.

Regarding Iraqi security forces, General Petraeus said, "I see tangible progress. Iraqi security elements are being rebuilt from the ground up… And Iraqi leaders are stepping forward, leading their country and their security forces courageously…There has been progress in the effort to enable Iraqis to shoulder more of the load for their own security, something they are keen to do…There are reasons for optimism. Today approximately 164,000 Iraqi police and soldiers… are performing a variety of security missions. Equipment is being delivered. Training is on track and increasing in capacity. Infrastructure is being repaired. Command and control structures and institutions are being reestablished. Most important, Iraqi security forces are in the fight."

Regrettably, General Petraeus made these encouraging statements in a September 2004 Washington Post article. Three years later, and four and a half years after the invasion, Petraeus sat in the Capitol and emphasized the need to limit U.S. troop withdrawals from the current 164,000 to a still-troubling 130,000 in July of 2008, 18 months after The Surge began. I maintained internal order without any foreign troops. Therefore, as benchmark number two, President Bush has ordered me to get it done my proven way. That will naturally entail killing and capturing many more than the 1,500 insurgents a month the Americans have been bragging about. On the other hand, I think I'll be able to kill fewer Iraqi civilians, though that is not something the president and I worry much about.

Privately – unfortunately, we have no pictures of this – President Bush and General Petraeus were verily in tears as they said, "Saddam, you not only controlled the Iraqis, you held off the Iranians in a war that killed hundreds of thousands on each side. You know what benchmark number three is: neutralize the Iranians. No one does that like you."

So I'm most honored to again be allied with my old American comrades, who are manly enough to admit that I long achieved what they haven't been able to and never will, not without me. Now General Petraeus won't have to frenetically repeat, as he did during the 2003 invasion, "Tell me where it ends." It ends with an Iraqi strongman kicking ass until democracy is internally generated.

Bush Analyzes Intelligence Report on Iran

I'm not relieved the National Intelligence Estimate recently revealed with high confidence that Iran had stopped its nuclear weapons program in 2003. That doesn't change my opinion: Iran was dangerous, is dangerous, and always will be unless Americans and the international community continue to respond to my warnings that Iranian nukes could lead to World War III and a mushroom cloud over your home. Some said I'd kept talking weeks after learning about the NIE. That's not true. I just got that report last week. It must've been filed away somewhere. No matter when I read it, the report strengthens my position by proving the Iranians were trying to make nuclear weapons from the late 1980's to 2003. Remember, they only stopped because of my resolve in rallying the world against them. Economic punishment was severe and soon to increase. The Iranians knew I'd bomb their facilities, too. I believe in attacking people before they attack us.

Reporters and others are asking why the world should trust me now, after intelligence failed me in Iraq and in the 2005 National Intelligence Estimate that Iran would soon be ready to launch. Iran hasn't become a peaceful nation. It's still a country with a radical regime that wants to enrich uranium. And I think they're trying. Fools keep whining the Nuclear Nonproliferation Treaty grants Iran the right to enrich for peaceful purposes. I think we could've reasoned with the Iranians before satanic Ahmadinejad became their president. He's a dangerous man who wants a "peaceful" program so Iran can someday sneakily switch and start making nuclear weapons.

I'm not going to permit that on my watch. And despite his close business relationship with Iran, President Vladimir Putin of Russia agrees. We just discussed this in person. I told Vladimir all about the latest NIE. We're good men and understand that "Iran has a sovereign right to have a civilian nuclear power program. What they don't have is our confidence they should be able to enrich uranium so those plants would work. Why? Because they had a covert weapons program they did not declare and have yet to declare."

It's my divine duty to prevent them from enriching uranium, the most essential process in building nuclear weapons. They've already got the missile delivery systems. Building bombs wouldn't be that tough once they get revved-up uranium. Don't worry. I know how to handle it. I'll keep the Iranians worried about my aerial assault against their nuclear facilities, and lots of other targets, until I leave as president. Then Dick Cheney and I will start Nuclear Power Production, Incorporated, and we'll sell the Iranians enriched uranium they need for peaceful purposes, and later collect the spent fuel. That'll keep them honest.

2008

CHAPTER 6

Delighted after Five Years in Iraq

On this day five years ago I launched Operation Iraqi Freedom, a farsighted and generous commitment I knew would lead not merely to the liberation of Iraqis but oppressed people everywhere on earth. I can now state – as I incessantly have – what no one can creditably deny: we're winning in Iraq. We've been winning all along. We removed a regime that threatened all free nations. Granted, Saddam Hussein couldn't have destroyed us under a mushroom cloud then, as I'd claimed, but that doesn't matter because if I hadn't attacked the Iraqis would've eventually made nuclear weapons and either used them or sneaked them to terrorists. Saddam used to punish people for simply wishing he were gone. I removed him because of what he wished as well as what he really had done.

The world immediately improved after the defeat of this horrifying man whose henchmen built "children's prisons and torture chambers and rape rooms where Iraqi women were violated in front of their families." I was right to hang a villain who filled "fields with the remains of innocent men, women and children." And I am determined as I tell you that though this war "has been longer and harder and more costly than we anticipated…it is a fight we must win." We're confronted by terrorists who were "seeking to stop the advance of liberty in the Middle East and to establish safe havens from which to plot new attacks across the world." I don't let liberals bother me with complaints Al Qaeda wasn't linked to Saddam and now exists in Iraq only because I attacked and occupied. I don't believe that.

This is what I know: The Surge – a phrase we prefer to escalation, which smells like Viet Nam – has been working. "A little over a year ago, the fight in Iraq was faltering. Extremist elements were succeeding in their efforts to plunge Iraq into chaos." Our strategic reinforcements routed the terrorists in their strongholds, denied them sanctuary elsewhere in the country, and better protected the Iraqi people. "In Anbar, Sunni tribal leaders had grown tired of Al Qaeda's brutality and started a popular uprising called the Anbar Awakening… Soon similar uprisings began to spread across the country. Today more than 90,000 concerned local citizens are protecting their communities." Instead of Arabs joining Al Qaeda to drive us out of Iraq, as the terrorists expected, Arabs are rallying to us to drive Al Qaeda out. These efforts are also aimed at Shia extremist groups armed and financed by Iran, a country I'm still trying to find a way to strike.

First, there's more "hard work to be done in Iraq. The gains we have made are fragile and reversible. But on this anniversary, the American people should know that since The Surge began, the level of violence is significantly down, civilian deaths are down, sectarian killings are down, and attacks on American forces are down. We have captured or killed thousands of extremists in Iraq... (And) The Surge has done more than turn the situation in Iraq around – it has opened the door to a major strategic victory in the broader war on terror."

We must consolidate our gains. We must not run or Al Qaeda will "regain lost sanctuaries, fomenting violence and terror" in many nations I'd rather not attack.

Iraqi Woman Rebuts Fifth Anniversary Speech

George W. Bush claims he's winning the war in Iraq, and that's pitiful as it is tragic. This is what he calls victory: thousands of teenage girls, and widows like me, fled into hills around Damascus and sold our bodies. Now my pimp says he plans to shoot any Iraqi, including Prime Minister al-Maliki, who tells Syria to send us home. We can't go back. They'll kill us, and before that they'll rape the women and stuff men's genitals into their mouths. I won't believe Bush really considers this winning until he vacations in an unguarded villa on the bank of the Euphrates.

Bush Rebukes Arabs on Israel's 60th Birthday

You probably know I recently got back from the Middle East. That's my area of expertise, and the region I'm determined to transform. It's hard work because a couple hundred million Arabs still aren't doing what I tell them. I shared that spirit in a speech to the Knesset of Israel on the sixtieth anniversary of the birth of that peaceful democratic nation, which "was the redemption of an ancient promise given to Abraham and Moses and David – a homeland for the chosen people of Eretz Yisrael." I don't think much about a few hundred thousand Palestinians being herded off their land and penned in camps sixty years ago. Far more important then was that "David Ben-Gurion proclaimed Israel's independence, founded on the 'natural right of the Jewish people to be masters of their own fate.'" I haven't read it myself but others have and told me Ben-Gurion also felt his people should be masters of the fate of Arabs in this area.

I don't like to hear that stuff. It doesn't fit my world view. I instead told the Knesset that Israelis "have forged a free and modern society based on the love of liberty, a passion for justice, and a respect for human dignity. You have worked tirelessly for peace." I can't believe some Arabs were upset by that. I'm disappointed they don't know that "free people should strive and sacrifice for peace… We also believe that nations have a right to defend themselves and that no nation should ever be forced to negotiate with killers pledged to its destruction." Applause rocked me after that line.

I heard more clapping when I said, "Some (like Barack Obama) seem to believe that we should negotiate with the terrorists and radicals, as if some ingenious argument will persuade them they have been wrong all along. We have heard this foolish delusion before. As Nazi tanks crossed into Poland in 1939, an American senator declared: 'Lord, if I could only have talked to Hitler, all this might have been avoided.' We have an obligation to call this what it is – the false comfort of appeasement, which has been repeatedly discredited by history."

I know some of my freedom-hating enemies have compared me to Hitler, but they are really the ones like him, and Barack Obama, a weakling like Neville Chamberlain, does not understand history or international relations or war and wants to negotiate away the liberty of Israel and of all democratic people. I think Obama would let Iran have nuclear weapons. If he'd had his way, I couldn't have liberated Iraq and established a flourishing democracy there. With Obama we'd have had a nuclear arms race between Saddam Hussein and Mahmoud Ahmadinejad. Thank God John McCain is willing to stay in Iraq a century if necessary but is confident he can deliver an "ingenious" victory in about four years. That'll be a victory my actions made possible.

I may not have been good at reading the short-term future the last seven years but sixty years hence, on the one hundred twentieth anniversary of Israel, I'm positive that "from Cairo to Riyadh to Baghdad and Beirut people will live in free and independent societies." This transformation "is possible in the Middle East, so long as a new generation of leaders has the courage to defeat the enemies of freedom, to make the hard choices necessary for peace, and stand firm on the solid rock of universal values."

A few days later in Egypt I told the Arabs that meant they've got to get rid of dictators who throw the opposition in jail. They don't need to do that. Look at me. I either get a majority behind me, as during the hysterical buildup to my 2003 invasion of Iraq, or, like now, ignore the majority in America that thinks I'm a failure and our occupation of Iraq a crime and a disaster. That's not what it is. Despite maybe a couple hundred thousand Iraqis getting killed so far, my actions have been humanitarian and I've got the moral authority, bestowed by God, to tell the Arabs to "release their prisoners of conscience, open up their political debate, and trust their people to chart their future."

They'll struggle till they do what I say.

President Bush Strives to Ensure Iraq's Future

As so often demonstrated I more than anyone understand what Iraqis need. And, using my executive authority, I recently tried to give it to them. This accord would have bypassed a weak and indecisive United States Congress and, among other generous commitments, given the Iraqis fifty-eight permanent American military bases, twice what we've got there now, ceded us the right to define hostile aggression against our friend and ally, guaranteed our control of their otherwise vulnerable airspace, and granted immunity from prosecution for our troops and military contractors. Shortsighted people in the Iraqi government have rejected many of my proposals and received predictable political backing here and in Iran.

I'm amazed people call me inflexible and dogmatic and worse. While the Iraqis were complaining about my desire to permanently occupy and colonize them, I was already improvising in ways one Iraqi critic called in "harmony" with their desires. I want the Iraqi people to be happy. If they are, that'll mean they're free and democratic and safe. They can only be that way with my help. Just tell me. What's the problem? Okay, we agree private contractors won't be immune to Iraqi law. And after hostile engagements, we'll hand over prisoners to Iraqi officials. We also guarantee our troops will operate only with knowledge and approval of the Iraqi government. Regarding their fear we want to use Iraq as a base to attack unnamed other countries, don't worry. We swear we won't do that.

Many Iraqis, as well as the usual whiners elsewhere, are saying if Iraq really is free and democratic, then they have the authority to simply order U.S. troops and contractors to go home. Listen carefully as I tell you the majority of Iraqi politicians don't want us to leave unconditionally. Many simply want to confine us to our bases, while they control internal security, which they feel they can, and remain ready to protect them from external threats, which they know they can't handle. Others say go ahead and leave but be ready to return if someone attacks Iraq. That's unreasonable and why I'm trying to establish a legal status of forces agreement to help my successor avoid difficulties. Once I've done that I can retire confident in fifty years historians will be arguing whether I'm most like Lincoln, Franklin Roosevelt, or Truman.

Bush Embraces Missiles

I'm a reasonable guy. I understand other nations need sovereignty, too. They just don't need as much as we do. They'll get more sovereignty when I think they're ready. As commander-in-chief of the democratic world, I have a sacred obligation not merely to protect free people from terrorists but from themselves. Right now I'm having a heck of a time convincing Iraqis, as well as the Czechs and Poles, what their vital interests really are.

Those Iraqis still don't understand, despite my endless warnings, that a timetable for withdrawal of our liberating American troops would signal weakness to the terrorists and allow them to hunker down in safety until we left and then unleash destruction upon Iraqi security forces which, even after our billions of dollars in weapons and training, still are not capable of defending themselves against a much smaller and lightly-armed group of insurgents I call terrorists because I don't understand the distinction and hope you don't either. Despite that, many Iraqis now boast they can handle internal security and won't tolerate any permanent U.S. bases unless they control them. Some Iraqi wisecrackers have offered to establish military bases under their control in the United States. They don't understand we have an inalienable right to maintain bases wherever we want. Guantanamo Bay isn't sovereign Cuban territory. It's ours. The world would crumble if we abandoned our bases. We're going to stay forever in Korea and Europe.

Later this summer General David Petraeus will explain to them how many U.S. troops can leave and when. I don't see a big change when a guy like Muqtada al-Sadr, the radical Shiite, says he'll order his forces to attack if our troops haven't retreated. What I'm really trying to do is ensure conditions in Iraq never dictate a complete U.S. withdrawal. We've got to have a safety net for the Iraqi people, and I like keeping our forces next to Iran.

At the same time, Secretary of State Condoleezza Rice and I are trying to pound sense into Czechs and Poles. Though the Czech Republic just signed an agreement letting us establish an antiballistic radar station on their territory, two-thirds of the Czech people oppose that and so do almost half their politicians. They also have yet to agree to the essential deployment of U.S. troops at the radar site. The Poles are also clueless, so far refusing to agree to accept ten interceptor missiles unless we provide billions of dollars in security guarantees and enhanced air defenses arrayed against the Russians, who aren't happy, either. For goodness sake, this system is also designed to protect them. It'll take out terrorist missiles launched from Iran and other such countries in the region. One of them could be Iraq, if we don't stay.

Taliban Thanks President Bush and Congress

Dear President Bush and the Congress of the United States,

We are writing to you, the once omnipotent leaders of the United States, to thank you for making possible the restructuring, growth, and fatal effectiveness of the Taliban. Following the Al-Qaeda led and Taliban-abetted assault on your country seven years ago, you counterattacked Afghanistan with remarkable speed and skill, and routed every enemy you found and forced many others to run and hide. You were propelled by the outrage and political will of your country and, indeed, much of the world. We thought our comrades would either be crushed in a cave or shot down on a road. Instead, you did what we could not possibly have achieved: you not merely saved us, you launched us into an era of modernity.

Your wild goose chase into Iraq, if I may use an American colloquialism, diverted energy from us onto those you had already vanquished in 1991 and thereafter contained. This both astonished and delighted the Taliban, and we resolved to embrace your gracious reprieve. Whereas we'd once been perceived, in Afghanistan and abroad, as bearded and uneducated religious zealots more fixated on sealing minds and shrouding women than becoming an effective political entity, we changed. Though we still sell opium, and intimidate, maim, or kill as many enemies as possible, we now also have computers and websites that instantly offer our version of truth faster than you can post yours. Young men who join us receive bonuses and, as we grow and improve weaponry, we're developing our own governmental departments of defense, economics, and the judiciary.

Our return to power is inevitable, and we believe you in the West understand the primary reason: all foreign occupiers must eventually go home. You are, in fact, undermining your position by recklessly launching missiles that kill civilians here as well as in Pakistan. What would Americans do if foreign soldiers on your soil were murdering your citizens? What would your response be if deadly missiles were being fired from neighboring Canada or Mexico? For you that would be intolerable. And, let me assure you, it is no less so for us. Empathy has not been a hallmark of American foreign policy, has it?

Regarding this principle we acknowledge the new Taliban must someday promise, and demonstrate by unequivocal action, that it will never permit Al Qaeda to operate in Afghanistan. The United States cannot win a war here but neither can it tolerate a festering threat such as that manifesting on September 11, 2001. We fifteen thousand Taliban fighters, whose numbers will continue to increase, do not want to face two hundred thousand or more Americans in our homeland. We are no longer as primitive as you think. We will negotiate. We will make a deal. This, regrettably, is not imminent since you are committed to the inept "democratic" regime of President Hamid Karzai. He will not much longer be in power, whether he's removed by you or by us. In the meantime, our Taliban task is to kill fewer Afghans and more American and NATO troops, and use new technology to promote our emerging philosophy that if you don't occupy us we won't let your enemies stay here either.

Sincerely,

The Taliban

Flying Shoes

I'm an athlete with lightning reflexes so couldn't help ducking when that Iraqi journalist jumped up calling me a dog and fired one then another shoe at my head. I wish I'd stood there and taken both soles in the chops. That would've even more strongly proved what I said it anyway did: Iraq is a democratic society where journalists and everyone else can freely express themselves. Imagine what would've happened to that guy if he'd targeted Saddam.

You know who took care of him and is responsible for starting and then maintaining our whole effort which is just about ready to deliver victory. "What victory?" cry the defeatists. "Scores of thousands of Iraqi civilians have died since we invaded in 2003." That's what it took to start stamping out terrorism around the world. Don't pay attention to polls that paint me a warmongering fool. I'll leave office with Iraq an oasis of peace, if you discount those bombings, and the opportunity for us to also transform Afghanistan into a special country.

Taliban Oscar

Most honored we are to accept an Oscar for our cinematic tour de force "Whip the Whore." Unlike other documentaries, this one you've probably seen. It's a rage in Pakistan as well as the satanic West where half-naked females parade in public, defile themselves before marriage, and rebel thereafter. We in the Taliban denounce these perversities and resolve to protect our sacred creatures: they shall not attend school and be thus exposed to ravenous males or unholy women; they shall refrain from reading and writing; they shall not have access to the carnal temptations of electronic media; they shall never work nor, we pray, even dream of it.

These decrees we make as warriors whose long and dirty beards enhance extraordinary toughness you witness in "Whip the Whore." Perhaps you can't see our heads swathed in stinking garments like robes of the KKK, but do not believe we fear revealing ourselves. We are brave men who wrestle a teenage wench to the earth and, as she wails, thrash her with a hard rubbery scepter. Some allege she had spread her legs before marriage, others that she declined a tribal leader's demand of marriage. It matters not which offense was committed: she is indeed fortunate not to be buried to her neck and stoned. We merciful men of the Taliban whip with restraint that, ultimately, permits the chastened one to rise and run away. A mortal threat she will be no more.

EPILOGUE

Bush on Saudi Men and Women

Remember that great photo a few years ago of me holding hands and smooching with King Abdullah of Saudi Arabia, who looked cool with black mustache and goatee glistening under his white keffiyeh headdress. He's one of the richest oil guys in the world and always nice to me. The Saudis are my friends. And they're yours too. I don't care fifteen of nineteen 9/11 hijackers were Saudis. What does that prove? Remember, the kingdom had banned Osama bin Laden from his native land long before 9/11. That proves we were right to attack Iraq instead of the Saudis.

All those times I preached about the transformative power of democracy marching across the Middle East, I wasn't talking about my petro buddies. For them I wanted and still want the status quo, which will give us all the cheap oil we want. Okay, the oil ain't cheap anymore but we'll still get all we want, at least all we can pay for, which is plenty since the Saudis and Chinese will loan us the money to buy it.

Mostly, I'm writing today to remind you that in a speech from November 2003 I stressed that "stability cannot be purchased at the expense of liberty" and that as long as "the Middle East remains a place where freedom does not flourish, it will remain a place of stagnation, resentment and violence ready for export." What these principles meant, along with my invasions of Afghanistan and, especially, Iraq, is that I am the father of democracy in the region. I say this not to brag but to stress that freedom is God's gift to humanity.

So please quit writing me letters about Manal al-Sharif recently being imprisoned for eight days in Saudi Arabia because she was driving a car. Don't act like I'm unaware Saudi Arabia is the only country in the world that bans women from driving. I also know that Manal al-Sharif has a U.S. driver's license and was accompanied by her brother, to prevent her from doing something immoral out there by herself.

I want you to know that my wife, Laura, has a driver's license and so do my pretty twin daughters. I believe women should drive, but until the petro boys give the okay, Saudi women will have to continue to deal with travel restrictions that also concern buses and appearing alone in public and either stay home or pay a few hundred bucks a month for a private driver. I don't care for these laws but keeping women at home can be a good idea. That way they won't "be flogged in the women's marketplace as a model and a lesson," as Saudi cleric Sheik Ghazi al-Shermri wants to do to Manal al-Sharif.

For the record, I've never held hands with or kissed Ghazi al-Shemri, and wouldn't unless I were still president and needed oil.

Saddam Comforts Americans

Despite their unconscionable betrayal I am poised to help the Americans when they inevitably return to my Iraq, which has ordered them out, a laudatory move on the surface but ghastly when analyzed. If not for my need to hide, where I cannot yet reveal, I could have explained, and in fact did long ago state, that I was an ideal bulwark against the gathering Iranian colossus, yet the Yankees shattered my formidable military that had so gallantly battled the Ayatollah Khomeini's hordes during the Eighties.

Still, I am determined to join the Americans in saving the Middle East. We both want stability and fear the same demons including Prime Minister Nouri al-Maliki, a traitor who lived in wartime Iran and helped it attack his native land. I guarantee he'll soon unabashedly jump into Iranian arms, and would have to even if disinclined.

This unholy duo will form an axis with bloody Syria, embracing Bashar al-Assad or, if he falls, getting tight with Shiite successors. An emboldened Syria will then devour Lebanon and threaten Israel not merely with an unbroken alliance from the Mediterranean to Iran but will squeeze the Jews, and thus America, from the south as enraptured Egypt resumes a national union with Syria, creating a five-country force of more than two hundred million jihadists led by nuclear Iranians lurking to launch a strategic knockout.

Only I can galvanize the Iraqi people and thus help America prevent my nation from becoming the first tumbling Middle Eastern domino in a sequence guaranteed to ignite regional and probably international conflagration. For my vital help I demand simply a return of my authority and all palaces staffed by a new generation of liberated women.

Sam Retired in Florida

Sam's a helluva good guy I occasionally play golf with. He's good looking and swarthy and impresses me the confident way he carries himself despite being a beginner shooting high scores on the best courses in Florida.

"What kind of work did you do?" I recently asked

"My business. What kind of work you do?"

"You know I'm a plastic surgeon."

"Good profession. You Cubans have so much here."

"Castro's fault," I said. "He's an incompetent dictator

"Right, most of them don't know how to do it."

"Where'd you say you're from?"

"Nowhere, like last time you asked."

"Just curious."

"Middle East."

"Guessed that. But where?"

"Anywhere.

"Plenty trouble there," I said.

"I'd stop that."

"How the hell?"

"Kill protestors."

"That's not working. Look at Syria. Someday the United States might intervene."

"Keep blood inside borders. Maybe your double won't hang."

Sources

Bush Debates Ahmadinejad - President Ahmadinejad's Letter to President Bush, May 9. 2006; Stratfor, March 21, 2006; The New Yorker, April 17, 2006; Harper's Magazine, July 2006.

Saddam Hussein's Final Interview – <u>MoreOrLess.net.au</u>

About the Author

George Thomas Clark is the author of *Hitler Here*, an internationally-acclaimed biographical novel, *The Bold Investor*, *King Donald*, *In Other Hands*, *Paint it Blue*, *Tales of Romance*, *Death in the Ring*, *Obama on Edge*, and *Echoes from Saddam Hussein*.

Clark also follows the news and sports, exercises daily (albeit delicately), collects contemporary art, enjoys independent movies, and travels to places (most recently Madrid, Mexico City, Quito, Guanajuato, and Aguascalientes) where he can socialize in Spanish.

The author's website is <u>GeorgeThomasClark.com</u>